"This is all wrong. Being here will ruin everything we've already done."

Behind Enemy Lines

INFINITY RING

Behind Enemy Lines

Jennifer A. Nielsen

SCHOLASTIC INC.

To Noah, who will one day hold the world in
his hands. There is a price for greatness,
for standing out from the crowd. It isn't easy,
but in the end it's always worth it.
—J.N.

All rights reserved. Published by
Scholastic Inc., *Publishers since 1920.*
SCHOLASTIC, INFINITY RING, and associated logos
are trademarks and/or registered trademarks of Scholastic Inc.

Library of Congress Control Number: Available

ISBN 978-0-545-48462-6
10 9 8 7 6 5 4 3 2 1   13 14 15 16 17

Cover illustration by Michael Heath
Map by Jim McMahon © Scholastic Inc.
Book design by Keirsten Geise
Back cover photography of characters by Michael Frost © Scholastic Inc.

Library printing, December 2013
Printed in China   62

Scholastic US: 557 Broadway · New York, NY 10012
Scholastic Canada: 604 King Street West · Toronto, ON M5V 1E1
Scholastic New Zealand Limited: Private Bag 94407 · Greenmount, Manukau 2141
Scholastic UK Ltd.: Euston House · 24 Eversholt Street · London NW1 1DB

EUROPE, 1943

ATLANTIC OCEAN

NORWAY
SWEDEN
FINLAND

NORTH SEA

Aberdeen

GREAT BRITAIN

DENMARK

BALTIC SEA

IRELAND

NETHERLANDS

EAST PRUSSIA (GERMANY)

London

Berlin

POLAND

ENGLISH CHANNEL

BELGIUM

GERMANY

BAY OF BISCAY

Paris

LUX.

CZECHOSLOVAKIA

SWITZ.

AUSTRIA

HUNGARY

FRANCE

ITALY

YUGOSLAVIA

PORTUGAL

SPAIN

Madrid

ALBANIA

Huelva

MEDITERRANEAN SEA

SPANISH MOROCCO

ALGERIA (FRANCE)

GREECE

SICILY (ITALY)

MOROCCO (FRANCE)

TUNISIA (FRANCE)

N
W   E
S

0   300 MI
0   500 KM

LIBYA (ITALY)

Hit and Run

RIQ WARPED into their new reality with a hard landing on the pavement. Grumbling loudly, he did a quick check to see if anything was broken. For some reason he had a stick in his back pocket, evidence of their recent adventure with Sacagawea. It was split in two, but that wasn't the break that worried him. He was sore where he'd landed on one knee, and knew he'd have a nasty bruise soon. When he'd joined the Hystorians, nobody ever warned him about the more painful parts of the job.

"Are you guys okay?" he asked Dak and Sera. But when he received no answer, he jumped to his feet and looked around. Where were they?

"A little help, please!"

That was Dak's voice, but it took a minute for Riq to find him. When he did, he groaned in disbelief. Dak and Sera had landed above him on the awning of a building. They might as well have landed in a pillow factory. He reached up to offer them a hand down, but Sera only grabbed the bar of the awning and used it to swing herself to the ground.

"Showing me up now?" Dak asked with a laugh. "Okay, I've got this." He took hold of the same bar but instead of gracefully rolling off the awning, he lurched down like a falling sack of flour and got his belt caught on the pole.

Between bursts of laughter, Riq managed to say, "It's amazing you survived without me for so many years."

"Hey, the last time I fell onto an awning, I got down just fine," Dak said defensively.

Which made Riq wonder exactly when and how something like this had happened to Dak before. It wasn't during their time travels. But he decided not to ask.

Riq grabbed the kid's belt, but it also took Sera's help to yank Dak free. When he fell, he landed on them both and they all crashed to the ground. Riq was pretty sure he bruised his other knee in the fall. That figured, because once again Dak had something soft to land on. Him.

Once they'd gotten back to their feet, the friends brushed themselves off while they looked around the area, a quiet town with small shops and friendly looking stores, all closed for the night.

"It's late," Sera said. "I feel like we should be tired, but to us, it's still just another day in the American frontier."

Riq sighed. For a long time, he had been disconnected from anything he *should* be feeling. "It's all relative," he said. "The time, the day of the week, seasons. No matter what the clock says, we sleep when we're tired and eat when we're hungry. . . ."

"Well, I'm both." Dak licked his lips to emphasize the hunger. "Let's explore the town and maybe we can find a place to stay and get something to eat. There has to be some cheese here somewhere."

The streets were narrow and wound in seemingly random directions. Riq's eye immediately sought out written words, to get a sense for where they might be. Many of the buildings in this area looked old, but cars lined the roadside and an occasional phone booth or mailbox occupied the sidewalk.

"We're in the twentieth century," Sera said as they started walking. "And somewhere in Europe, I think? I wish the SQuare had told us where and when we were going, and not just the coordinates to enter into the Ring."

Riq pointed to a shop sign on their left. *"McGregor and Sons, Butchers,"* he read. "Written in English."

"We're in Aberdeen, Scotland," Dak said. "April 21, 1943. Smack dab in the middle of World War Two."

Riq hated to admit it, but sometimes Dak was pretty good at figuring things out. He started to say so, then stopped when he looked over.

"What?" Dak had his nose buried in a half-crumpled

newspaper. Even from here, Riq could see its name, *The Aberdeen Press & Journal*. No doubt the date was printed somewhere right below it.

"Yeah, you're a regular Sherlock Holmes," Riq said.

"If you mean that I'm good at gathering clues for my brilliant deductions, then I take that as a compliment!"

"Okay, Sherlock, then figure out why we're here." Riq looked around. "Who has the SQuare?"

With one hand still on the newspaper, Dak reached into his pants and pulled out the electronic tablet, then held it out for Riq.

"Ew, no!" Riq had never understood why the kid had to carry it in his pants.

"I'll take it," Sera said, stretching out her hand. "It's been acting funny ever since I had to take it apart in Baghdad, so I'll probably have to tinker with it anyway."

The three of them huddled beneath a streetlight and Sera powered on the device. The screen was slower to come on than usual, which worried Riq. Even in the twentieth century, technology was still very basic. The best computers of this era filled entire rooms and were only capable of simple math. Where were they supposed to get another SQuare if this one failed?

He knew the answer to that: the future. In fact, the Hystorians had already told them they would have to return to the future for a new SQuare before they could fix the Prime Break that had started it all. But Riq wanted to put off that trip as long as possible. He'd interacted with his own ancestors several Breaks ago, and he was terrified of facing the consequences of his actions. Especially if the consequences meant that when he returned to the twenty-first century, he would no longer exist.

Sera pounded on one side of the device and words faded onto the screen. One word, actually, and she leaned in to see it better.

"It must be broken," she said. "We only have one piece of the code."

"What's the word?" Riq asked.

She shrugged. "Run."

Riq folded his arms, wondering what sort of clue could be embedded in that word. "Run? Yeah, that could mean anything."

"On this date, in Aberdeen, that means only one thing," Dak said. "RUN!"

He bolted down the street with Riq and Sera on his heels. They hadn't gotten far before Riq detected the faint buzz of engines coming toward them. Airplane engines, and plenty of them.

"Bombers!" Riq cried.

Dak paused long enough to turn around. There was fear in his eyes, and Riq couldn't help but follow his gaze. Silhouetted against the night sky were the forms of several planes, flying low enough that the black Nazi swastika was clearly visible, outlined in white on their tails. A shudder went through him just to look at it.

"It sounds like people screaming," Sera said, covering her ears to block out the horrible noise.

"Those are sirens on the planes," Dak said. "It's psychological warfare, meant to scare people."

"Because bombings aren't scary enough?" Sera called back.

"Everyone was scared of the bombings," Dak called over his shoulder. "The German air force was one of the strongest in the world at this time."

"Stop yelling history facts and run faster!" Riq said.

Dak's retort was drowned in another siren, this one coming from nearby. The earsplitting sound pierced the night, warning the sleeping town of the raid.

And then the planes were upon them.

Dak dodged toward a street on his left, but from the corner of his eye, Riq saw a plane drop something in that direction. He grabbed Dak's sleeve and yanked him the other way. Sera screamed as another bomb landed down the street on their right. Glass shattered nearby, and the entire wall of a building crumbled to the ground.

There might have been people in that building, Riq thought.

"C'mon!" Sera made a run for a church straight ahead of them.

"No!" Dak shouted. "No, I've seen pictures of that exact church . . . afterward."

Other people were swarming into the streets by then. Half-dressed men and women carried children in their arms or hurried them hand in hand down the streets. The children wailed as explosions echoed throughout the town in a deadly fireworks show. Riq, Dak, and Sera found themselves overtaken and forced to move in the direction of the crowd. But Riq had no idea where the crowd was headed and didn't like the feeling of being wedged against so many panicked bodies. When he saw a way out, he grabbed Dak and Sera and pulled them into a side street.

They ran straight into a squadron of soldiers rushing to help what people they could. Riq and Dak backed against the wall in time, but Sera was slower and was knocked to the ground. One of the soldiers stopped, a lanky young man with an easy smile and red hair shaved close to his head. He reached out a hand to help Sera to her feet.

"Ye're not from Aberdeen." His eyes scanned their clothes and then flicked to the SQuare in Sera's hands. "Where's ye fowk?"

"Our families?" Riq responded. While Sera brushed herself off, he said to the soldier, "We're on our own, very far from home, and we need shelter."

"My name is Cadet Duncan Shaw," the soldier said. "I'll help you lot, but keep edgy for the bombs."

Duncan steered them down an alley. Riq looked up at the high stone walls and thought if a bomb landed up there, it'd bring the surrounding buildings down on their heads before they had a chance to escape.

"Where are you taking us?" he asked.

"Bomb shelter." He hurried them forward until they came to a small metal structure with a rounded roof, half buried in the ground. "On yer knees now."

He practically pushed Sera to the ground. Dak and Riq crawled into the shelter right after her. Something exploded behind them, and they crawled faster. Duncan followed them, and only seconds later the sound of granite walls and other debris falling into the alleyway blew into their shelter, along with dust and small bits of rock.

"It's a gubbing from the Nazis tonight!" Duncan said.

"Gubbing?" Dak mouthed to Riq.

Riq sighed. "A beating."

"My translator isn't picking up on some of the words," Sera whispered to Riq. "Maybe it's broken, too."

"It's working fine," Riq said under his breath. "It just considers this English."

They sat there a moment in silence, in a space barely big enough for six or seven people. Riq wondered if anyone else would follow them into the shelter, but no one did. Then Dak started to squirm. By now, Riq recognized why. Dak was thinking about some history factoid that just had to be shared, whether anyone wanted to hear it or not.

"Spit it out," Riq said. "You look like you'll hurt yourself if you don't."

Dak grinned. "The German planes are impressive and all, but the really interesting ones were the British

Spitfires. Did you know they were painted pink? That allowed them to fly almost invisibly below the clouds at sunset. Imagine that—pink warplanes!"

"The only warplanes that interest me right now are the ones over my head," Sera said. "Why couldn't we warp into someplace quiet for once?"

Duncan sighed and leaned forward with his hands at rest on his knees. "Aye, it's as I thought. I ken what ye need. Sit down, lads, and let's have a blether."

"A long talk?" Riq rephrased it for Sera's benefit only. Dak could figure it out on his own. "Talk about what?"

"Ye're a very long way from home, eh? Measured in years, not miles."

"How did you know—" Sera started to ask.

But Duncan only smiled. "I recognized ye at once. I'm yer Hystorian."

2

The Hystorian's Challenge

DAK SHARED a glance with Riq and Sera. He saw his own question reflected in their eyes: Could they trust Duncan? Ultimately, though, he figured Duncan couldn't be SQ, or else he'd have pushed them into the path of the bombs, not saved them. Then again, they had been tricked before.

Dak decided to take the risk. "If you're our Hystorian, what do you think has gone wrong here?"

Duncan rolled his eyes. "Do ye hear the bombs? The pelter in the streets? C'mon, lad, everything is wrong here!"

But Dak only shook his head. "World War Two was the most destructive war in world history. Millions of people died and the world was never the same again. But even though war is terrible, that doesn't mean history has gone wrong."

In fact, Dak was tired of having history go wrong. Everything he understood about the world was based on his knowledge of the past. Having to doubt the history he knew felt like walking across thin ice and wondering when it would all break apart.

"I ken what you mean," Duncan said. "But the Allies must win this war. If we lose, then it's not only the Nazis who win. It's the SQ also."

Dak closed his eyes. Every student learned about the Second World War in school, and of course, he always knew more about it than the teachers, who usually let him take over the lesson for the class. Not only did this war spread fighting to all corners of the globe, and launch weapons capable of destroying entire cities, losing the war had also shattered the idea of freedom — real freedom — around the world.

On one side were the Axis powers: Germany, Italy, and Japan. Germany was led by Adolf Hitler, someone Dak considered one of the greatest villains of history. Hitler's goal was to build an empire for the people he felt deserved to live, namely those of his own race and ethnicity. Even thinking of him, and the millions who were killed under Hitler's orders, Dak felt sick to his stomach.

Much of the world rose up to fight against the Axis powers, but the Allied powers, as they came to be known, were led by the United States, Russia, and Great Britain. That included Scotland, now under air assault.

"But nobody wins this war, not really." Sera

nudged her best friend with her elbow. "Believe it or not, Dak, when you talk, I do pay attention sometimes."

Dak's eyes flew open. "What do you mean *sometimes*?"

She only shrugged a halfhearted apology.

"If you listened to *everything*, then you'd know the most important part," Dak said. "The Axis and Allied powers beat each other into the ground, but a winner does emerge in the end. Because all the destruction creates a void. It leaves a hole for an organization that has been waiting hundreds of years for the right opportunity."

Riq jumped in. "Shortly after the end of World War Two, the SQ openly revealed itself to the world, offering peace, safety, and progress. The world took hold like a drowning man to a rope. But instead of fulfilling its promises, the SQ only brought tyranny and fear."

"Aye, it's as we thought," Duncan said. "The Hystorians believe the Allies must win this war, or else there'll be no stopping the SQ." Then he pushed out his chest to better display his uniform. "It's why I joined the Royal Navy. I've got to fight, do me part. But we need someone to change the direction o' things. You three."

Sera shook her head. "Three kids change the direction of a world war? That's crazy! There's no way."

They paused for a moment while an explosion went off very close to them. Something crashed against the side of their shelter, denting the metal behind Riq. They all scooted in closer to the center and waited for the noise of falling debris to fade.

When it did, Duncan said, "It won't be easy for ye, but it is possible."

"How?" Riq asked.

Duncan turned to Dak. "Ye're a dead clever lad for history, right? Tell me, what do the Allies need so they can win?"

Dak snorted. Asking what he wanted for dinner was a harder question than that. "Germany and Italy were very well defended," he said. "If the Allies are going to win this war, they have to break through those lines."

"It's like a soccer game," Riq said. "You can play defense all you want, but you'll never win unless you go on the offense to score a goal."

"Yeah, Riq," Dak said. "Major world wars are just like soccer games. Just *exactly the same.*"

Riq and Dak both grunted as Sera kicked each of them in the shins. *Speaking of soccer, that was pretty good skill,* Dak thought. She'd kicked two different targets at the same time, and pretty hard, too.

"I ken your point," Duncan said. "Aye, the Allies must break through to Germany and Italy. The best place to do it is the island of Sicily."

"Yeah, good luck with that," Dak said. "Guess who else knows how important Sicily is? Germany! Hitler's got that place so well defended, the Allies could lose everything if they attack there."

"How can we help?" Sera asked.

Duncan looked around a moment as if checking for any eavesdroppers, which Dak found odd since they were the only ones in the shelter and the air raid was still going on outside. It wasn't really a good time for eavesdropping. When Duncan was satisfied, he said, "He's no Hystorian, but my best mate works in London, in Room 13 of the Admiralty. He told me of a plan there. I've sworn to keep it stum, but I think I should tell ye lads."

To hear better, Dak leaned so far forward he almost lost his balance. He loved the idea of a secret plan!

"What do ye lads think of being spies?" Duncan asked, smiling.

As far as Dak was concerned, that sounded great. He started to tell Duncan about how espionage went back to the earliest days of recorded history, but was cut off by the sound of a woman crying for help out in the alley. Duncan poked his head out the door. "You lot stay here, and be cannie. I'll go help her!"

He ran into the night while Dak, Sera, and Riq watched from the door, hearts in their throats. He got the woman safely beneath an arched doorway, but as he ran back toward the shelter, another explosion went off and rock toppled from the skies above, filling the alley like an avalanche of destruction.

Riq pulled Sera and Dak to the far end of the shelter, and they watched as large chunks of granite filled the small doorway until, only seconds later, it was completely blocked and everything went silent.

Riq's Secret

FOR THE longest time, Sera didn't speak. She couldn't even begin to think of the words that should be spoken in such a moment. The air raid seemed to have ended, or at least, the explosions stopped and the sound of engines passed. But there were no other sounds either, and certainly not Duncan's cheery voice.

Finally, Sera whispered, "Do you think he's . . . ?"

She looked over at Riq, who slowly shook his head. "There's no way he survived that."

The three friends all dropped their eyes to the ground and shared a moment of silence.

"He died a hero," Dak said at last. "And he told us enough to get started here. We have a chance to save a lot of lives."

"Yes, but how?" Sera asked. "The Hystorians can't honestly expect three kids to conquer Sicily."

"We're not conquering anything," Dak said. "Duncan asked if we could do spy work. I think that means we're supposed to work behind the scenes. If we succeed, the Allies will do the conquering."

"So this will be easy," Riq said dryly. "I suppose we could just start asking around to see if anyone is hiring underage spies."

"That's not helping!" Sera sighed. "Listen, we still have the SQuare. It'll give us the clues we need." She looked around. "Where is it?"

Sera looked at Dak, who looked at Riq, who looked back to Sera. Suddenly, they were all talking and pointing fingers. Sera had given the SQuare to Dak when they ran into the crowd. Dak had dropped it to help a child that had fallen, but Riq had picked it up. He had tossed it into the shelter when they climbed in, but none of them remembered seeing it since they got inside.

Then Dak frowned and pointed to the entrance. "There it is."

"There it *was*," Sera mumbled. Sure enough, a corner of the SQuare could be seen in the entrance, crunched beneath tons of granite, wood, and bricks. Even if they could pull it out—and they couldn't—it was totally destroyed.

Sera blinked back the sting in her eyes. She wasn't going to cry, not about *this*.

"If you had the right materials," Dak said, "you could—"

"Somehow I doubt there's a wide availability of lanthanum or neodymium in 1943," Sera said, thinking of the metals she would need to properly repair the SQuare.

"It's okay." Riq seemed eerily calm. "We knew this moment would come. We need a new SQuare. You and Dak have to go home and get another one."

Riq was right—a trip to the future was the only way to get another working SQuare. But she couldn't ignore how Riq had left himself out of the plan.

"Why not you?" Sera asked. "People back home will want to see you."

"How would you know?" Riq snapped.

Sera still didn't understand, but her eyes darted to Dak, who was staring at Riq and slowly nodding as if he had figured out some big secret. Whatever it was, it couldn't be worth breaking the three of them up.

Dak caught Riq's eye. "Okay, so where do we go once we get home? Last time we dropped in on the ol' HQ, we were blindfolded."

"It's not hard to find if you know where to look," Riq said. "Just outside of the city limits is an old shoelace factory."

"Tiny Worm Shoelaces?" Sera smiled. "Yeah, my uncle drives past that place every day on his way to work. He always makes fun of it."

"Everyone does." Dak scoffed. "Seriously, who wants to wear shoelaces that look like worms? So the headquarters are near there?"

"No," Riq said. "That *is* the headquarters. Tiny Worm

Shoelaces is an anagram, a name lame enough to keep the public and the SQ away, but to let all Hystorians know they're—"

"Welcome," Sera finished. Once she knew it was an anagram, unscrambling the letters was easy. "Hystorians Welcome. That's what the building's name really says."

"Exactly!" Riq turned his attention to Sera. "You and Dak should find Arin there, and a lot of other people who can load a new SQuare for you."

"We'll all go together," Sera said. "It's too dangerous to leave anyone behind."

Riq pressed his eyebrows together and for a moment looked as if he was about to say something. Then he shrugged and said, "If we're going to be spies, someone has to stay here and start creating a cover story for us. I'll do that."

"We have a time machine," Sera said. "We can build the cover story when we come back."

"Trust me, it has to be this way." Riq's tone was more insistent this time. "Listen, you can warp back to London one week from today's date. That'll give me time to get there and start figuring things out."

"We could meet at the Tower of London, right at noon," Dak said. "Fascinating place. A lot of beheadings happened there, including a couple of queens. It was also a zoo—"

"No!" Sera felt angry that Riq wasn't budging, and

that Dak wasn't helping her. "We're not leaving without Riq. What if he gets into trouble with the SQ?"

"I won't," Riq said. "Tower of London, one week from today. I'll be there."

"Plug in the coordinates to take us home," Dak said to Sera. Then he turned to Riq. "Stay safe, dude."

Sera reluctantly entered the coordinates, but she had no intention of pressing the button to send them away until she convinced Riq, and now Dak, that they must all stay together.

Dak put his hand on the Ring and shared a grim look with Riq that Sera didn't like. Whatever secret Riq had, it was big, and she was sure by now that Dak knew what it was.

"Take my hand," Sera said to Riq. "Whatever is wrong, we'll fix it together."

"See you in a week," Dak said. And then before Sera could stop him, he pushed the button that would send them away.

Sera was yanked into the warp still yelling at Dak and holding out a hand to Riq. Dak had a firm grip on her at first, but as they were pulled along the time stream he cried out in pain, and nearly lost hold of her and the Ring. Now it was Sera's job to grip Dak tightly. She wouldn't lose him to time the way he had lost his parents.

After what seemed like a particularly long trip, Sera was spat out of the warp onto solid ground. The usual shudder ran through her, but she shook it off and turned her attention toward Dak. He was curled into a ball beside her and visibly shaking.

"Wh-wh-what's hap-pening t-t-to me?" Dak said.

"Oh," Sera said softly. "You've just had a Remnant."

A Homecoming Welcome

SERA HAD experienced hundreds of Remnants in her life, some of them so awful they literally made her sick. They always left her cold and often in tears. Having become so familiar with them, it wasn't hard to recognize when her best friend had just experienced his first one.

Lying on the ground, Dak continued shivering like they'd just landed in the middle of an arctic winter.

"If you're st-st-still mad at m-me," he said through chattering teeth, "feel fr-fr-free to gloat."

She *was* still angry with him. He'd been wrong to leave Riq behind, and never should've forced her to leave that way. But it was hard to stay angry while he looked so pathetic.

Sera crouched down beside him and put a comforting hand on his shoulder. "You never get used to it, but at least the feelings pass pretty fast." The Remnant was probably made worse by the stresses of time travel, which were already hard enough. At least he'd stopped shivering.

Dak rolled to a sitting position and wrapped his arms around his legs. "I'm sorry, Sera. I never understood before. Not really."

"I wish you didn't have to understand now." Then she smiled and bumped his side with her elbow. "But this is the point of what we've been doing. We're fixing things."

She had expected Dak to respond with his usual positive attitude, or at least something playfully sarcastic.

But now he only looked at her with eyes that had become hollow and hopeless. "Not this time, Sera. You said that Remnants are a feeling that something has gone wrong. That what you see with your eyes isn't what you feel is true." He turned away and shook his head. "Well, something's definitely wrong. I think coming back here was a mistake."

"We didn't have any choice. If we don't get a new SQuare, we'll have no way of knowing what else needs to be fixed."

"Then let's just get it and leave as fast as we can."

That was what they *should do*, yes. But Sera still felt haunted by what she'd seen in the Cataclysm. She longed to go home, just for a minute, just to check that everything there was okay. And maybe better than okay. Sera had learned, to her horror, that her parents were destined to die in the Cataclysm. But that meant they should be alive *now*. What if they were at home waiting for her? Or . . . what if they weren't? To go there and find her home as empty as before, it would almost feel like she was losing them all over again.

Dak shuddered, drawing Sera's attention back to him. "Can't you feel it, too, Sera? This is all wrong. Being here will ruin everything we've already done."

She squinted against the rising sun behind him. "How can being in the present ruin the past?"

"I don't know! But it does, okay? Something's going to happen that—" He stopped, as if choking on his own sentence.

"That what?" He didn't answer and Sera asked, "What's with you and Riq all of a sudden? Do you know why he wouldn't come back with us?"

"I think so." Dak shrugged. "He's been acting weird ever since 1850, with Harriet Tubman. And I think I figured out why." Then he turned to Sera. "But that's for him to talk about, not me."

"Is it bad?"

Dak nodded. "Yeah. If I'm right, it's pretty bad."

"And your Remnant, the one you just had—"

Dak got to his feet and began running down the quiet street. He called behind his shoulder, "Let's just get the new SQuare, okay?"

Sera ran after him, but her mind was racing even faster. She knew how hard it had been to tell Dak what she had seen in the Cataclysm. And Riq clearly knew something that kept him from coming here at all. What had Dak just experienced that he didn't want to share with her?

It only took one look at the Hystorians' headquarters to know it was completely destroyed. Maybe a tornado had driven right through the building, or maybe this was all that was left after the SQ had invaded.

That was a cheery thought, Dak realized. To not know the difference between an SQ attack and a natural disaster.

"When are we?" he asked. "I mean, how much time has passed here since we left?"

"It's only been a couple of days," Sera said. "I figured if we came back much later then there would be too many people looking for us. We did just sort of up and disappear."

Yeah, Sera would think of things like that. If it had been up to Dak, they would've come back early enough to save his parents, or at least in time to warn the Hystorians about the SQ attack on their headquarters. But maybe bumping into their old selves would create some huge time paradox. Probably not a good thing.

Still staring at the ruins ahead of them, Sera said, "The Hystorians won't be in there anymore. How far do you think it is from here to your house?"

Dak shook his head. "We're not going back there."

"Riq said the Hystorians watched your parents' lab. If we go there, they'll find us."

"Maybe the SQ watches it, too. I'll betcha Riq didn't think of that!"

Dak knew he'd scored a point there, but the look on Sera's face told him that she understood the real reason for his protests. He didn't want to go home, not yet. Wherever and *when*ever they'd traveled, Dak'd been too busy figuring out puzzles, dodging Time Wardens, and living the world's history to think too much about his parents. To wonder if they were still all right. And to worry about what would happen to them if he failed.

But if he went home, that was all he'd be able to think about. Losing them once was hard enough. He didn't want to go through that again.

"We don't even have to go inside," Sera told him. "Just make sure the Hystorians know we've come back. Then they'll give us a new SQuare, and after a quick stop at my house, we'll hurry back to 1943 again. Easy-peasy. No problem."

Dak caught the part about a visit to her house, but he wasn't going to argue with that. He knew she had questions that made her want to go home just as strongly as he wanted to avoid his own. So he began trudging along beside Sera. "Okay, we'll go to my house. But the one thing I'm learning about time travel is that there's *always* a problem."

A New Traveler

IF IT really only had been a couple of days since they left, then Dak and Sera had barely missed some truly harrowing events. A gap in the earth had split open along Main Street and was so wide in some places that entire cars had been swallowed into it. Several windows of their school were boarded up with a *CONDEMNED* sign across the entrance. And the theater near Dak's home now had an uprooted tree lodged upside down through its roof. Where the current show's name had once been *The Farthing Family's Music*, the *h* in *Farthing* was now missing from the billboard.

Dak snorted out a laugh and pointed to the sign. "Look, Sera, now it says —"

"I can see what it says."

"That would make some interesting music, all right."

Sera only rolled her eyes while Dak continued laughing. "I need to hang out with more girls," she mumbled under her breath.

Dak sighed as they turned into his neighborhood. "Just trying to lighten the mood. I gotta say, this was not the welcome I was expecting. Where is everybody? And shouldn't things be a little bit better than when we left? I mean, we've done a pretty amazing job of fixing Breaks so far."

Sera nodded silently. This was almost harder than when she'd seen the Cataclysm. Because as awful as it was now, she knew it would only get worse. The streets were entirely empty, but eyes peered back at them from windows and doorways. She wanted to scream at the people to run, but where could any of them go? Everything, everywhere was going to be destroyed.

"We have to succeed," she said to Dak in a hushed voice. "No matter how tired, or scared, or worried we get —"

"We won't give up," Dak finished for her. "I agree."

There were no signs of any Hystorians when they approached Dak's house. Not that Sera had expected any, but it would've been nice to have some idea of how to get another SQuare. His parents' lab seemed quiet enough, though the door was slightly ajar. Maybe the Hystorians really were watching this place.

"Do you have the Infinity Ring programmed already?" Dak asked.

"Yes." No matter how badly she wanted to go home, the devastation had convinced her it wasn't a good idea. For all she knew, the Cataclysm could kick off at any moment. And besides, Sera didn't like the way Dak had looked after his Remnant. The minute that SQuare got into their hands, she wanted to leave for someplace safer. *Like the battlefield of a world war,* she thought wryly.

"Then let's get the SQuare and go," Dak said. "All we need now is a Hystorian."

"I'll bet Arin left us some sort of message inside the lab," Sera said. "Maybe even a code, like we always get on the SQuare, to tell us where to go next."

Dak's eyes darted left and then right as if he was uncomfortable. "Why don't you go check that out? I'll, uh . . . keep watch out here."

This time, Sera didn't push. She knew he didn't want to be reminded of his parents any more than he had to be. And maybe he was still shaken by the Remnant he'd experienced. Unfortunately, Sera understood how that could feel, too.

So she nodded and said she'd be back in a minute or two.

It was dark inside and the lights didn't flip on when she tried them. That wasn't a big surprise. That earthquake along Main Street likely destroyed much of the city's power grid. But the Smyths' private generator, which kept their computers running, was still humming along. She could see the dim light of the screens at the far end of the room and used it to guide her way forward.

"Hello?" a woman's voice called.

Sera froze as a chair that had been facing the computers slowly spun her way. She squinted, hoping to see whoever was seated there better, but with the only light coming from behind the chair, the person was cast in shadow.

"Sera, is that you?" the voice asked. "What a relief to see that you're still safe! Is Dak here, too?"

"He's waiting outside," Sera replied. "Who are you?"

"We met at the Hystorians' headquarters. I hoped you'd come back here."

Sera stepped forward a little closer. The voice did sound familiar, but everything had happened so quickly before they escaped the headquarters, it was hard to place it. She didn't think it was Arin's voice, or Mari's. What other women had they spoken to that day?

"I'm sorry, what was your name?" Sera asked.

The woman leaned forward and, for a moment, Sera thought she got a glimpse of an angular chin. But then the woman reclined and her face disappeared again into the shadows. "You haven't completed your mission, Sera. Why are you here?"

"Our SQuare was destroyed during an air raid in World War Two."

"And is the Infinity Ring okay? You have it with you?"

Sera clutched the satchel in her hands. "It's fine. We just need a new SQuare and then we'll hurry back there."

"Certainly. I have one right here. Come on over and I'll get it for you."

The woman returned to face the computers and plugged a SQuare in, probably to update it with the most recent data. Still, Sera didn't walk any closer, and she kept an eye on the exit, just in case.

"Marq is okay, too," Sera said casually.

"Who?" The woman remained facing away as she worked on the SQuare.

"Marq—the Hystorian you sent to help us with languages."

"Oh, yes . . . Marq. Fine young man."

Sera's mouth pinched together. Whoever was seated in that chair, it was no Hystorian. All of them would've known it was Riq who came with them, and that there was no Marq.

"There now, I have your SQuare ready," the woman said. "But there've been some big changes since you left. Call Dak in and I can explain them to you both."

"Sure." Sera already had her fingers wrapped around the Infinity Ring. She would get outside, grab Dak's hand, and get them out of here. The explanations could come later.

Only Sera had barely turned around before Dak burst through the door. "We have to go right now!" he cried. "There's SQ coming!"

"Actually," the woman said, "we're already here!" And with that, she stood and her face was fully lit by the computers around her. Sera saw the fierce lines of her jaw, hard and square. The red glow of the SQuare in her hand deepened the bloodred tones of her hair, and as the woman came closer, her oily black lips whispered, "It will be less painful for you both if you just give me the Ring."

"Tilda!" Dak hissed.

Sera remembered Tilda all too well. The woman was an ambitious leader within the SQ, intent on clawing her way to the top. She had led the raid on the Hystorians' headquarters, a raid in which good people had been killed, and she had obviously been waiting for their return.

"Now don't go anywhere, Sera," Tilda said. "Don't you know how much you've worried your parents?"

Sera froze. Dak clutched her arm as if he wasn't sure whether she'd bull-charge the woman or faint on the spot.

But Sera didn't move. "Where are they?" she asked through clenched teeth.

"Mommy and Daddy?" Tilda laughed, a humorless, throaty laugh that screeched like nails on a chalkboard. "Oh, they're fine . . . for now. But they have a lot of explaining to do, and they won't be slipping away from us again."

"Explaining?" Sera stepped forward. "About what?"

Now Sera felt Dak tensing at her side. "Has the SQ done something to her parents?" he asked.

"Oh, so you kids don't know the truth?" Tilda's laugh turned dark and sinister. "Sera, your parents *are* SQ! They work for me!"

"No!" It was everything Sera could do to keep from attacking Tilda in that moment. "You're lying!"

The voices of the SQ agents entering Dak's backyard carried into the lab. Soon, there would be no escape.

"You let my parents go!" Sera cried.

"No, Sera, *we* have to go," Dak said.

Sera turned to look at him, then felt Tilda's hand on her arm, pulling her back. Dak lunged for the woman, knocking her down.

"The SQuare!" Sera yelled. It was still in Tilda's right hand, waving wildly in the air.

Dak put one hand on the Infinity Ring, and then stretched enough to grab the SQuare with his other. He wrenched it from Tilda's grip and said, "Get us outta here!"

At that moment, the doorway was filled with SQ thugs, yelling and pushing to be first through the door to capture the two young time travelers.

Sera had her thumb on the Infinity Ring's button. "Hold on tight!" she yelled at Dak. Instantly, she felt time grab on to her gut and yank her into the warp. She opened her mouth, but realized someone else was already screaming. She looked over at Dak, whose face was vibrating so hard he'd shut his eyes as if to keep them from being sucked out of their sockets. But his mouth was clamped shut, too.

So who was screaming? Sera turned her head the other way.

Before they left, Tilda had been holding the SQuare

with her right hand. Sera had noticed that. But she had never thought to check for where Tilda's left hand had been.

It was on the Infinity Ring. Tilda was traveling with them through time.

The Trout Memo

RIQ HAD come early to the Tower of London, where he was supposed to meet Dak and Sera. Maybe there was no point in coming early. No matter when they left, they would arrive at the precise time that Sera programmed into the Infinity Ring, and not one minute before.

This time and place weren't too bad for him to navigate on his own — after all, he'd made it to London without any trouble. But the truth was that he'd gotten used to having Sera and Dak with him on these adventures. They were all friends now; even Dak was, though neither of them would ever admit it. But it was something more. Dak and Sera had become like family to Riq. And he hated the thought that one day, they would finish these missions, save Earth from the Cataclysm, and then go home. Eventually, they would have to leave him behind for good.

But not today. Riq straightened his spine and paced for the twentieth time around the gatehouse that marked the entrance to the Tower of London. He had managed to get a job as a translator for the British Royal Navy. It was a civilian job, and the information he could access was so low-security that he could've put it on a billboard with flashing lights and no one would care. But it did get him inside the Admiralty building where the British spies worked, and that was a good start. Dak and Sera would have to be impressed with that move.

Where were they, already?

Somewhere in the distance, the chimes of Big Ben bonged out the change of the hour. One. Two. Three. Wasn't it time for them to show up? Six. Seven. Eight. It felt like each chime was longer than the last. Then, finally, ten and eleven.

Just as the final chime sounded, with sparks coming from nothing but empty air, Dak and Sera tumbled into existence. And then a third body rolled through. Tilda!

Riq actually stumbled backward. Were they crazy? Why would they bring Tilda here?

Dak and Tilda seemed to be fighting over a SQuare, but Tilda was also fighting with Sera to keep a hand on the Infinity Ring. Riq dove between all of them and earned himself a hard kick to his chest and someone's elbow in his eye. He pushed between them again until Sera finally rolled free with the Infinity Ring and Dak separated on the other side with the SQuare.

"You miserable brats!" Tilda growled. "Do you really

think you have any chance of winning? Don't you know how strong we are here? This is where we took over the world!"

"What are we going to do with her?" Dak asked.

"We have to send her back, obviously," Sera said.

Riq didn't bother asking how they would do that. It'd be nearly impossible when none of them wanted to risk letting her anywhere near the Ring. That could be a fatal mistake.

He knew Tilda better than either of his friends did. As a child, he'd thought of her as a bogeyman — he'd already learned six languages before he could bring himself to say her name out loud. Then, as a young man, he'd studied her, as all Hystorians did. She was the most dangerous person alive, and vicious beyond words. Most Hystorians believed that the SQ would loosen its grip upon the world if only they could be convinced that the Cataclysm was real and that it was coming. But Tilda was driving the entire planet toward the Cataclysm and it seemed like she wanted to step on the gas pedal to make it happen sooner.

Then Riq remembered something else about Tilda. She came from the future. A future that their actions had already changed.

"Do you know who I am?" he asked her.

Tilda hadn't expected that. She stood there, recovering from her first warp through time, and blinked at him.

"Do you know who I am?!" He yelled the question

this time, lunging forward, gripping her arms and shaking her.

"Oi, you there!" A policeman on the street behind them had noticed them surrounding Tilda, had heard him shouting at her. Riq could only imagine how this must look.

"Run!" Sera cried.

Dak started to protest that they couldn't just leave Tilda, but Riq and Sera grabbed each of his arms and dragged him off. The officer pursued only a few steps before he returned to Tilda, who was doing a fabulous job of pretending she had been the victim.

"Yeah, helpless little super villain," Riq muttered when he glanced behind them. "That man had better not look her straight in the eyes, or I bet he turns to stone."

They ducked into a narrow alley to catch their breath, stow the Infinity Ring and SQuare, and brush themselves off.

Sera turned to Riq. "Do I even want to know what that was about?"

"Do I even want to know why in the world Tilda was with you?" he shot back. "What happened in the future?"

"I don't want to talk about that," Sera snapped, then eyed Dak. "Not ever."

Dak turned his obvious frustration back to Riq. "Maybe you've had it easy resting here for the last week, but for Sera and me that was three trips through time in just a few hours with an aerial bombing, a nice bomb-shell of news, *and* an SQ attack in between."

Riq hadn't been relaxing these past few days, but it certainly wasn't anything compared to what Dak just described. Still, when Dak bent over with his hands on his knees, Riq did consider giving him a push to the ground. Just a little one.

"Sheesh, sorry I asked," Riq said.

"Sera, I get it. I do." Dak had turned to face Sera, and his voice was low, as if he didn't want Riq to hear. Riq kicked at the ground, but aimed his ears in their direction to absorb every word he could. "My parents made mistakes, too."

"Really? And are their mistakes going to destroy the world?"

"Well . . . no."

"Then you don't get it." She pushed past Dak and said, "Let's just figure out what to do now. Are we going back for Tilda? Well?" Dak didn't say anything and, with the mood Sera was in, Riq wasn't about to be the first to speak. Sera folded her arms. "Someone answer me!"

"Okay." Dak glanced back toward the Tower of London. "Maybe it's better if Tilda is stuck in this time for now. At least she's not at home causing even worse damage. Without an encyclopedic knowledge of history, how much harm could she do?"

"And you got a new SQuare," Riq said.

"Tilda had it, not the Hystorians." Dak handed it to Sera. "I think you'd better check it out before we trust anything it says."

Sera made a face, then took it and started pushing buttons. "It's password protected, just like the first one was. I think she must have been trying to hack into it when we dropped in on her." She typed in a word. "The password is *password*, just like before. It's booting up now."

Riq reached into his bag. "Since we have a few moments, maybe you can both change into some clothes that don't stand out so much. Sera, I have a special surprise for you."

Sera looked up from the SQuare and narrowed her eyes as if she wasn't sure whether he was serious or teasing her. Riq pulled two sets of clothes from the bag, one in each hand.

He held up his right hand first. "Here we have a pretty polka-dot dress. Very nice." But he saw that Sera was already eying his left hand and a smile was spreading across her face.

"Pants!" she cried. "Girls *finally* wear pants here?!"

"It was a growing trend in the forties," Dak said. "Pants were more practical when so many women were going to work for the first time, to help the war effort."

"Not now, Dak!" Forgetting her bad mood, Sera thrust the SQuare back onto her friend's lap and yanked the pants and sweater from Riq's hand, then ran deeper into the alley. "If anyone comes back here while I'm changing, I'll hurt you. Pants!"

Riq chuckled to himself. "I knew she'd like that."

Dak pointed to the other clothes still in Riq's hands. "Good for her, but if you think I'm wearing the dress now, you're crazy."

Riq dropped the dress back into his bag and pulled out a pair of boys' pants and a shirt for Dak. "They're not fancy because everything is rationed here: clothes, food, supplies. But at least you'll blend in better than you do now." Once Dak had taken the clothes, Riq went back to his bag and pulled out some bread wrapped in brown paper. "I also figured you'd be hungry."

"Starving is more like it." Dak had a slice in his mouth even before finishing his sentence. "Is there any cheese?"

"Are you kidding?" Riq asked. "I had to scrub a grocer's floor just to earn that!" He hesitated a moment, then quietly added, "Was she mad at me, after you two went to the future?"

"She was mad at both of us," Dak said.

"But you know why I couldn't—why I can't . . . right?" Riq couldn't even say the words to Dak. It was hard enough just to think about his future, much less have to explain it.

Dak only swallowed the food in his mouth and said, "It won't take long for Sera to figure it out, too. We're here, when you want to talk about it."

That was good to know, but at least for now, Riq

still hated even thinking about it. He put his problems to the back of his mind when Sera reappeared in her new outfit. She did a high kick in the air and laughed, then told Dak to get changed next.

Once they were all ready, they gathered around the SQuare. Words had appeared on the screen.

TROUT:
HDMS2W EEMWTO LAAIHL PDNMEF

"Trout? Like the fish?" Sera groaned. "And the rest is gibberish. It could mean anything."

"And the number two is in the first word," Riq said, shaking his head.

"Maybe Tilda uploaded false codes after all," Dak said.

"I don't think so." Riq ran his finger across the screen. "This looks like Arin's handiwork to me."

"I was hoping it'd be written in Navajo," Dak said. "You know, because this is World War Two and the Allies used the Navajo language for a code. It's one of the only wartime codes in history that was never cracked by the enemy." He looked up at Riq. "You know Navajo, right?"

Riq shrugged. "A little. But there's a reason why Germany never cracked that code. It's a spoken language so, at least in 1943, there's no written record of it. Its details can change depending on the specific tribe, and a lot of words mean different things just by the way they're pronounced."

"So . . . that's a no, right?" Dak said.

"I know a little," Riq insisted. "At least enough that I was able to talk my way inside the Admiralty building as a translator. I only translate newspapers from other countries, so it's hardly top secret, but I figured if we're going to be spies, then we needed to get inside somehow."

"Exciting!" Sera said. "You're like James Bond with a day job."

"It's funny you'd say that," Dak said. "Because Ian Fleming, who created the James Bond character in the 1950s, *did* work for the British Secret Intelligence Service in World War Two. In fact—" Dak drew in a breath and grabbed the SQuare. "Let me look at this!"

Sera scooted toward Riq to give Dak room for whatever thought was working its way through his brain.

"Anyway," Riq said, "I've been working at the Admiralty—a lot of spy stuff happens there. Once they found out I knew so many languages, they've been very happy to have my help."

"Trout!" Dak interrupted. When he caught Riq and Sera staring at him, he added, "A few years ago, right at the start of the war, Ian Fleming wrote a list of ideas for how Britain might trick Germany, just like a fisherman lures in a fish. It was called the Trout Memo."

"But Ian Fleming only wrote spy novels," Sera said. "This is real-life spying."

"Maybe the reason he could write them is because he'd already lived them," Riq pointed out.

"Exactly! Do you have anything to write with?" Dak asked. Riq handed over a loose sheet of paper and the pen that he'd been using for work. Dak started writing immediately, then after a minute scratched out what he'd done and started over.

"Anyway *again*," Riq said, "maybe I could bring the SQuare's code in and ask some of their code breakers to look at it."

"For the love of mincemeat!" Sera said. "We can't tell anyone about this code. Time traveling brings a whole new meaning to the term *top secret*."

"Mincemeat!" Dak said. "Yes, Sera, you're brilliant! So am I, by the way. We're still waiting on Riq."

Riq muttered something back to him in a language their translators didn't pick up. In case Dak didn't know he'd been insulted, Riq added, "That was Navajo. And trust me, I got the meaning of my words exactly right."

To Riq's surprise, Dak only chuckled and went back to his writing. After a moment he looked up and announced, "I know the code. I just lined up the first letter of each word, then the second letter of each word, and so on. Six words, four letters each."

Sera and Riq looked to Dak's chicken scratch.

HELP DEAD MMAN SWIM 2THE WOLF

"Oh, good," Sera said. "That clarifies everything."

"You've made a mistake," Riq said, then chuckled. "What's an M-man? A mailman? Marshmallow man?"

Sera nodded, and with a snort of laughter, added, "Maybe it's the Muffin Man."

But Dak only shook his head. "Here's a tip for telling jokes, dudes. They're always better if they're funny." Then he stood and stuffed the SQuare into his pants. "The M-man is real, and it's the key to the Allies winning this war. C'mon, we've got work to do!"

Mincemeat Man

DAK WASN'T sure where he was going, only that he had so many ideas turning in his head that he needed to move, just to keep things flowing. Riq and Sera were on either side of him, and as they walked, he tried to explain the code.

"Hitler's first name, Adolf, means *wolf.* He used to call himself that sometimes, like a nickname."

"Charming," Sera muttered.

"And we have to help a dead guy swim to him?" Riq asked. "Because I'm not going near any dead bodies."

"Well, I'm not going anywhere near Adolf Hitler!" Sera said.

Dak stopped and turned to Riq. "When you were inside the Admiralty this week, did anyone ever talk about Room 13?"

"No, but Duncan mentioned it during the bombing, so I found it, but I'm not allowed to go inside. Why? What's in that room?"

"I sort of hoped that by now, you could tell me," Dak said.

"What?" Riq asked. "So, you don't know everything?"

Sera interrupted them. "Oh, for the love of mincemeat!"

Dak slapped a hand to his forehead as ideas moved like pinballs inside his brain. "'For the love of mince-meat'—exactly. You're always saying that, Sera."

She followed behind him as he started walking again. "I only say it when you two are fighting."

Dak grinned. "Like I said, you're *always* saying it. Anyway, I connected that with the word *Trout* in the code. M-man is Mincemeat Man. Mincemeat is a code of its own."

"Like mincemeat pie?" Riq asked.

"It's a code, not a dessert. I mean *mincemeat* as in slang for a dead man. You know, kaput, kicked the bucket, cashed out, toast. If you're dead, you're mincemeat."

"And some dead guy is going to save the war?" Sera asked.

"That was the plan," Dak said. "But in the history I learned, the plan didn't work. In fact, it backfired in the worst possible way. The Allies never recovered."

"Mincemeat!" Riq shouted. "Yes!"

"Could you say that louder?" Dak said. "The only way for everyone to know you're a spy is if you SHOUT OUT YOUR PLANS!"

Riq glared at Dak, then lowered his voice and said,

"Mincemeat—I've heard some people whispering about that. They got the body of a dead homeless person and dressed him up to look like a British officer. They call him Major Martin."

"That's him!" Dak stopped walking, this time because he realized he had no idea where he was going. Then he turned around to Riq. "The Allies are going to plant fake information about their next invasion on Major Martin. They want the Germans to discover it and believe what they're reading. But that's where they run into problems."

"What problems?" Sera asked. "The plan seems simple enough."

"To win this war, the Allies have to invade Sicily, right?" Dak's thoughts were still racing, but he tried to say everything slowly so he wouldn't have to explain it a second time. Or a tenth time, in Riq's case. "So their fake information has to do two things: First, it has to convince the Germans that the Allies are *not* going to Sicily."

"Even though they are," Riq said.

Dak nodded. "Right. But the Germans are going to see the Allies preparing for an invasion, so they have to make them think their target is actually somewhere else."

"Greece!" Riq said. "I heard people talking about Greece."

"I get it!" Sera said. "So the Allies want Germany to think they're invading someplace they're not, *and* that they're not invading somewhere they are."

"Yeah," Dak said. "Way to clarify that. Nice job."

"I still don't understand the problem," Riq said.

"In the history we learned, Hitler did get Major Martin's fake papers, but he never believed them. If Germany knows the story about invading Greece is a lie—"

"Then they know the story about *not* invading Sicily is a lie, too—" Sera said.

"So instead of tricking Germany, Mincemeat Man told them exactly where the Allies were going to attack!" Riq finished.

Dak folded his arms, satisfied with himself. "In our history—the wrong, SQ-twisted history—Sicily was a disaster for the Allies. The Nazis were ready for us, and we never recovered. The only way to fix things is to make sure the wolf—Adolf Hitler—believes Major Martin is a real British soldier carrying real plans for the invasion of Greece."

"How do we do that?" Sera asked.

Dak eyed Riq. "For a start, you have to get us inside Room 13."

8

The Secrets of Room 13

RIQ SIGHED. Dak had asked to get inside Room 13 as if that were something simple. As if they could just walk into the Admiralty, open the door, and peek at some of the most top secret plans of World War II. Sure, anyone could do that!

Then Sera pointed out that this was exactly the kind of thing they had to do in order to influence the war from behind the scenes. Easy for her to say. Two kids who were caught sneaking around would just get kicked out of the building. But Riq was older than they were, and he had a job there that involved sensitive matters of national security. If he was caught, could they put him in military prison? Could he be tried as a traitor?

It wasn't a pleasant thought, but Riq knew that Dak was right. They had to get into that room!

It took Riq most of the afternoon to wander the corridors of the Admiralty and its connecting buildings until he found an old, unguarded room in the basement with a window large enough for Dak and Sera to squeeze through. It was a good thing that *he* didn't have to come and go this way, but they were a little shorter and should be able to fit.

That was where he waited for them that night. What had started as a drizzle an hour before had turned into a heavy downpour. At any other time, that would've been a problem, but tonight, it was very good news. The rain would help camouflage Dak and Sera from the soldiers who patrolled the area, and hopefully lower the soldiers' guards a bit. Even so, he breathed a huge sigh of relief when the secret tap they'd devised came to the windowpane.

Riq inched the window open, which took more effort than he had expected. Who knew how many months or years—or decades—had passed since it was last opened?

A soaked Sera crawled through first, then Dak followed. They dripped on the floor so much it was as if they had brought the rainstorm inside with them.

"Next time, I'll stay in the warm building while you sneak through the rain," Dak told Riq through chattering teeth.

Riq had a nice response ready, but decided to save it for later. At least until Dak looked less like a wet puppy.

He started to close the window, but Sera said, "We should leave it open, in case we need to make a quick escape."

"Good idea." Riq frowned at the water now puddled on the floor, but decided it would dry long before anyone happened upon it. "Let's get this done."

He opened the door to the hallway, and then froze, certain he had heard a shuffle in the bushes outside the window.

Dak looked out, but only shrugged his shoulders. "Nobody except us is crazy enough to be out on a night like this. Must be the wind."

"C'mon, then." Riq led them into a narrow and dark hallway with low ceilings and worn paint. Outside, the rain seemed to have picked up speed. The pelter of drops echoed through the hallway, which masked any sound they might make, but it also made Riq nervous. It concealed any sound from an oncoming guard on his rounds, too.

Room 13 was marked clearly, but for a place that held such powerful secrets, it didn't seem to be anything special. Maybe that was the idea. If a German spy got in here, the last place he'd think to look for top secret plans was behind an ordinary door in a narrow basement.

Dak stepped forward and tried the door handle. "It's locked."

Sera shoved a hand in her pocket and pulled out some slim pieces of metal. "No worries. I've gotten pretty good at picking locks by now."

"Excellent," Riq said.

Sera went down on her knees and stuck the metal

pieces inside the handle. While she did, Riq explained to Dak how the few men and women who worked inside this room mostly kept to themselves and seemed very serious about their jobs. "But they're still just regular people," he whispered. "Everyday people trying to stop a really bad guy."

"Real spies don't have all the cool gadgets you see in the movies," Dak said, watching Sera struggle with the lock. "Though I sure wish we had a sonic screwdriver right about now."

Riq wasn't sure he got the reference, but he raised an eyebrow knowingly.

Sera continued fiddling for several minutes, all the time muttering to herself about the feel of the tumblers. Riq and Dak huddled in close to watch, and neither of them moved when she told them to back off.

"I can't . . ." she said. "This won't . . ." And then, halfway through a sentence that began "We'll never—" her eyes lit up and she exclaimed, "That did it!"

The lock clicked. Sera rotated it and pushed. "Let's go in," she whispered.

"Why don't we all go inside?" someone behind them said in an English accent.

All three kids turned, and sighed in unison. A tall man with wavy brown hair, prominent cheekbones, and bushy eyebrows was motioning them inside Room 13.

Once inside, he turned on the lights, then shut and locked the door behind him. Sera stood between the two boys, holding each of their hands. Or rather, locking their hands in a death grip. Riq would've pulled away, just to preserve some blood flow in his fingers, but Sera looked like she needed his support.

Okay, he was scared, too.

"Who are you?" Dak asked.

"Call me Anton." Then he chuckled. "I've always wanted to get inside the Admiralty, but I never thought three kids would make it so easy for me."

"So you're a spy?" Sera asked.

"I suppose you could say that." His eyes rested on Sera's sack, the one with the Infinity Ring inside, and Riq leaned closer to her to block Anton's view of it. Anton continued, "But I do not work for Britain or for Germany. They're too caught up in their war to see the bigger things happening in this world."

Riq jutted out his chin. "We don't care whose side you're on. We're not here to fight. We don't have anything to do with this war."

Anton's smile only widened. "Maybe not *this* war. But our war is even bigger, eh, time travelers?" He chuckled again. "That's right. We know what you look like now. There is no safe place for you in this era."

Riq's heart sank, and Sera squeezed his hand tighter, if that was possible. He cut a glance toward Dak and saw that the younger boy's eyes were fixed on some papers on a nearby desk. Riq suppressed a groan. Even if the secrets of the universe were on those papers, it wasn't the best time for Dak to be distracted.

"Do you have kids, Anton?" Sera asked.

The man looked her way. "What?"

Sera shrugged. "You're wearing a wedding band, and it's tarnished, so I bet you've been married a long time. Do you and your wife have any kids?"

"They live very happily here in London. Why? What's it to you?"

"It's nothing to me. Your kids are going to be fine," Sera said. "Because the SQ does win here. Big congratulations for that, by the way. You're about to get a lot of power and control, and pretty soon your children will have everything they want. But their children are going to have a lot to worry about. And your great-grandchildren—the ones who'll be around in the time we come from—they won't do so well at all."

"Why not?"

Sera continued. "The SQ is going to destroy the world—literally destroy it. I've been there. I've seen it for myself. If you don't let us go free, your grandchildren will face one disaster after another and your great grandchildren will not survive to adulthood."

Anton's eyes darted from one kid to the other. "You're lying."

Riq shook his head. "You're a Time Warden, so we know what your orders are. But we are the last hope for your family. What you choose to do right now can either save them, or destroy them."

Anton hesitated for a moment, and then frowned.

"You're lying. The SQ will *save* this world. In time we will control everything and everyone, and then there will be no more war or starvation or catastrophe. The woman in red has promised it."

Dak snorted, then went back to reading the paper.

Anton looked offended that his speech had failed to impress any of them. He stepped closer to Dak to get his attention. "I'm deciding whether to kill you and your friends. You might at least listen to me."

"Huh?" Dak looked up. "Sorry, I know you're under orders, but . . . wow." And his voice trailed off again as his focus wandered back to the papers.

Anton withdrew a pocketknife from his pants and opened the blade. "Tell you what. You all come with me, nice and quiet, and I'll take you back to Tilda. She'll know what to do with you."

"Hold on," Dak said. "I'll be finished in a minute."

"You'll come with me now!" Anton advanced with the blade angled toward Dak. "Or else."

"You wouldn't be threatening me if you knew how brilliant this plan is," Dak said. "But it's already in motion."

"What is?" Getting no response, Anton strode over to Dak and shoved him aside to look at the papers for himself. When he did, Dak picked up the heavy telephone from the desk and swung it at Anton's head. The man tumbled to the ground, unconscious.

"That was a great idea!" Sera said. "Getting him to look at the papers so you could attack him."

"That wasn't my plan," Dak said. "I really was reading the papers. I only thought of the telephone after he pushed me."

"So, what's on them?" Riq asked.

"We're almost out of time. They've already set sail with Major Martin's body, which means it'll wash up on the shores of Spain any day now."

"Why Spain?" Sera asked. "Why not send him directly to Italy or Germany?"

"That would be too obvious," Riq said.

"Spain is the perfect choice," Dak said. "Officially, they're a neutral country in the war. But unofficially, a lot of people in the Spanish government are on Germany's side."

"So we have to hope the people who get Martin's body support Germany and slip them the phony plans," Sera said.

"I think I know what we need to do about Mincemeat Man," Dak said, "but we're going to have to split up."

Behind them, Anton began to stir. "Tell us about it later," Riq said. "Let's drag this guy away from the top secret intelligence and dump him in some bushes before he wakes up!"

Split Up

THE NEXT morning, Dak stood with Sera and Riq at the ferry docks near London. He had explained to them everything he'd read the night before while in the Admiralty, but neither of them seemed too excited about the jobs ahead.

Riq handed scraps of paper to Dak and Sera with a phone number written on them. "That's for a pay phone near the Admiralty," he said. "Memorize the number, then destroy the paper, because we're spies now. I'll be at that phone every night at nine o'clock my time. Call once, then hang up, then call again. That's how I'll know it's one of you."

Sera shoved her paper into her pocket. "We'll both call every night. I don't like splitting up."

"Me neither," Riq said. "If the body is already on its way to Spain, I won't do much good here."

"If something goes wrong, we need someone here in London to warn the officials," Dak said. "You already have a job at the Admiralty, so it makes sense to keep you here, just in case."

"But what if Anton comes back?" Sera asked. "Or someone like him? I knew there would be SQ among the Axis powers. But the British are fighting for their freedom and survival. How can Anton really believe he's doing the right thing by supporting the SQ over the Allies?"

"Tilda lied to him," Dak said. "Just like the SQ lies to everyone else. She's made him believe that he's saving Earth from the Cataclysm."

"When they're the ones causing it," Riq added. "Don't worry about Anton. I'm sure it'll take him a few days to see straight again. You two just get your jobs done."

"I'll make sure Spain believes Major Martin is a British officer who drowned a few days ago in the ocean," Sera said. "Not a homeless man who died from rat poison a few months ago."

"I'll bet you know more about science than any of those coroners," Dak said confidently. "Fight science with science."

Sera bit her lip. "Riq and I have jobs that make sense. But why do you have to go to Germany?"

Dak didn't want to go behind enemy lines. But even if Riq and Sera did their jobs perfectly, none of it mattered unless Germany believed Martin's papers were real. Somehow, Dak had to get to Hitler.

"He was brutal," Sera said. "If Hitler suspects you're there as a spy—"

"Just do your parts right and maybe I won't have to do anything," Dak said quickly. "Mincemeat Man was a good plan, but everything had to fall in place perfectly for the plan to work."

"And if it doesn't, Hitler could have you sent to the concentration camps," Sera said. "Or even killed."

"I'm already dealing with the Cataclysm. If I can face that, then I can deal with Hitler." Dak shrugged, then a mischievous smile crossed his face. "That sounded pretty brave, right? We should remember that, for the book they write about me one day."

"You'd better go before I lose my lunch," Riq told Dak. "Besides, you don't want to miss your boat."

"You first," Dak said to Sera. She was going to use the Infinity Ring to warp to the morgue in Huelva, Spain, where Major Martin's body was expected to be taken. Traveling there by boat and across land could take a week or more, which would be too late.

Sera nodded and ducked into a thicket of trees nearby. She pulled the Infinity Ring from its bag, crouched low, and then pushed the button that would send her away.

Dak and Riq watched her go, and Dak was surprised to feel himself already missing her. It wasn't that he liked her, or at least, he didn't *like her* in that way, but things were never quite right when she was gone.

"Your turn," Riq said. "Is everything set?"

Dak hoped so. The easiest way to get into Germany was on a shipping barge. It had come from a neutral country and was only making stops at ports for businesses unconnected to the war. Dak had spent the entire morning talking a deck supervisor's ear off until he finally said Dak could have a job swabbing decks if he would just promise to stop talking.

"I'll try to call you tonight, from wherever I am," Dak said.

He started to walk off, then Riq said, "Quick question: plans like this in history . . . how often have they worked?"

Dak frowned back at him. "Something this big? Almost never."

With that, he waved good-bye to Riq and looked back at the area where Sera had disappeared, then ran up the gangplank and onto the ship. Once on board, he gazed over the railings of the ship . . . and then quickly ducked down low.

Tilda was on the dock, her head darting around like a pigeon's as she scanned the area. She was searching for him and Sera and Riq, no doubt. Carefully, Dak peeked back over the railing and groaned. Riq wasn't far from her, still watching Dak's ship as it sailed away. He was completely unaware of Tilda.

Tilda turned to a woman nearby to ask a question, and the woman looked Tilda over with clear disapproval before finally shaking her head and walking away. Only then did Dak pay more attention to her appearance.

She had on a tight red skirt and a shiny black jacket

with a bright ruby pin on the lapel. It was totally out of place for the time period, and practically screamed for everyone to notice her. With her red hair pulled up high on her head, she almost looked like a burning ember of fire. In fact, in many ways, Tilda reminded Dak of fire: Get too close, and you'd get burned.

Still on the shore, Riq gave Dak a final wave good-bye, then started to walk off. Tilda bobbed her head in Riq's direction, but Dak didn't think she had spotted him. Or had she? The ship was far from shore now. All Dak could hope was that Tilda was looking for three kids, and ignoring the single boy walking away.

By that time, the deck captain had begun shouting orders, and he put Dak to work cleaning the railings. It kept him busy, and that was better. The work helped keep his mind off of Tilda and the Cataclysm, the world war, and the fact that he was heading straight into the wolf's lair.

He scrubbed decks for nearly the entire day at sea, but was given a warm meal with the other crewmen that evening, shortly before the captain announced that the ship would soon be docking in Germany.

When the boat came into port, Dak ditched his mop and went down to ask if there were any boxes he could unload.

A crewman pointed to a small crate in the corner. "Those are goblets specially ordered in for Hitler," he said. "Carry them if you dare, but if you drop them, it'll be your head. Someone will be waiting for them on the dock."

Dak picked up the wood crate, which was heavier than it looked. Why couldn't people have discovered shipping in cardboard yet? That would've saved him a few pounds. But he kept it balanced in his arms as he walked across the gangplank and onto the docks.

"Are those the goblets?" The woman who asked was older, with stooped shoulders and graying hair. The wrinkles on her face were long and deep, but when she smiled, her eyes seemed warm and energetic.

"Yes." Dak felt relieved to hear his translator pick up the German language. It was the first time since he'd landed in 1943 that he'd needed to speak in a language other than his own.

"None of them had better be broken. They're for the Führer, you know."

"You work for Hitler, then?" Dak asked.

"I do kitchen work at a bunker in Berlin. Nothing more." She held out her arms. "Well, hand them over."

"The box is heavier than it looks," Dak said. "I'm worried you might drop them."

"And if I let you carry them for me, what would you want in return?" the woman asked.

"Just a ride to Berlin," Dak said.

She smiled. "It's a long drive. I'd enjoy the company. But you'll have to do more than carry this box to my car.

I'll also expect you to do all the unloading once we've arrived. If you work hard enough, maybe I can hire you. We need a good kitchen boy."

"It's a deal." Dak was quick to agree before this opportunity passed him by. He wouldn't be anywhere near a phone tonight to call Riq, but this was more important. For better or worse, he had just found his way into the heart of enemy territory.

10

Spy Class with Clauss

SERA ARRIVED at her coordinates in Spain with a pulsing migraine and with her body feeling as if it had not quite come back together. She wiggled her fingers to make sure they were still there, and was rewarded with sensations of hot electrical currents traveling from them along her arms and into her chest. *Forget the Cataclysm,* she thought. Time travel would destroy them much sooner.

Remembering the ways she had managed these feelings before, Sera backed against the nearest wall and forced herself to breathe, to just draw in a full gulp of air, and release it again. Slowly, the pain faded, but she promised herself that she would not use the Infinity Ring again until she absolutely had to. She doubted her body could take much more.

It turned out she had unknowingly backed up against just the right wall. The morgue entrance was only a few yards to one side, and from the other direction and around the corner, she could hear two men arguing. She flattened herself against the plaster and listened. With any luck, nobody would notice her there.

"You must let me see that body!" a man said. Even without the translator, Sera knew he was speaking in Spanish, but his accent was German. She hadn't realized there would be any Nazis here, but it seemed like a safe bet now.

The person who answered had a Spanish accent. "Clauss, the man inside this morgue is a dead British officer. You are a German — an enemy to that man. Why would I let you see him?"

Clauss lowered his voice and his tone became more desperate. "Doctor, you don't understand. I am quite well connected in Germany. There are people in my country who would do anything . . . *anything* . . . to get their hands on the dead officer's briefcase. I will pay you well if you only let me see what it contains!"

"I don't want your money, Clauss," the doctor replied. "Now you must excuse me. There are people inside who are waiting to begin." He rounded the corner with Clauss on his heels, then they both stopped when they saw Sera.

"Are you all right?" The doctor put the back of his hand against her forehead to check her temperature. Little did he know the reason for the sweat on her brow and flushed checks was worse than a simple flu.

Sera nodded calmly, but on the inside her pulse was racing. She had heard enough of their conversation to know that her real mission was more than just convincing Spain to accept Major Martin's fake cause of death. She had to convince Clauss, too.

"I couldn't help but overhear you just now. And I can help with the postmortem," she said.

"How?" The doctor's eyes narrowed. "A girl of your age has done a postmortem examination before?"

"Well . . . no." But Sera had read about them, and even sat in once on an autopsy performed at a local hospital, just for fun. But she hadn't gotten that close to the body and half the time her view was blocked by the doctors doing the procedure. "My name is Sera, and I'm very good with science. I can hand you tools, and record your observations. I know anatomy and chemistry, and I'm a quick learner."

The doctor nodded. "All right. I could use another set of hands, *if* you know when to stay out of our way. Come on in."

The doctor went inside, but Clauss grabbed Sera's arm and pulled her back. He was so thin he almost looked unhealthy, and had a high forehead and a face that looked as if it had been cut from stone. Not a single hair on his head moved in the light breeze. Either he used gallons of gel each day, or else his hair was cut from stone, too.

"Tell me everything you see in there," he said. "I'll pay you well for any information."

Sera shook him off. "How much?" Clauss wasn't

likely to trust her as a spy. But he obviously trusted in the power of a good bribe.

He withdrew a thick wad of money from his pocket and flipped through it. "That depends on what you tell me."

Sera felt like running away, or yelling, or doing nearly anything other than helping this man. But she was a spy now, and this was her one chance to convince Clauss she was on his side. She whispered, "If you meet me after the examination, I'll tell you everything I see."

Clauss studied her a moment, then leaned in and pinched her cheeks. "I'll pay you for information I can use," he said. "But if I find out you are lying, or holding back a single detail, then you are the one who will pay."

Sera wormed from his grip, then backed away from his threats and into the morgue. There were others in the room besides the doctor. A man in a British uniform stood there looking bored—did he know about Mincemeat Man, or was he just as confused as everyone else? Next to him was a man in a Spanish uniform who was holding a wet briefcase—Martin's, no doubt. He asked if they could hurry up, because he had already missed lunch. The doctor was working with a young attendant, and Sera thought she saw a resemblance between them—his son, perhaps? There was an American soldier, too, sitting in the corner and looking like he was about to be sick from the horrid smell in the room. None of them paid Sera much attention, except the doctor who handed her a clipboard and told her to write down everything he dictated.

And, of course, lying flat on a table was the guest of honor: Major Martin. Mincemeat Man, who was worse than dead. He looked like a full-on zombie, with sunken eyes, yellow skin, and knotted hands. Right then and there, Sera decided that she would grow up to be a physicist or a botanist or any scientist that didn't deal with dead bodies. Because this was just gross!

The attendant started by emptying Martin's pockets. Most of what he found was useless — just soggy old receipts, some cash, stamps, and two ticket stubs from a theater. Sera wondered why anyone had bothered to put all that into his pockets — none of it had anything to do with the fake plans.

But then she realized it wasn't about convincing the Germans that the plans were real. It was about making the Germans believe *Major Martin* was real. If they thought Martin was a real British officer, they'd automatically believe his plans. Major Martin wasn't supposed to be some unfortunate homeless person who'd been holed up in a freezer for the past three months. He was supposed to have been alive only a few days ago, doing the things living people did. All that stuff in his pockets was genius.

Next, the Spanish officer placed the briefcase on a table and unlocked it with an attached set of keys. Seawater dripped back onto the papers inside as it was opened, but that didn't matter — they were already plenty wet. On top of everything were a handful of envelopes with red wax seals over them. They looked very official, like secret military plans. Sera pictured Clauss outside, drooling in his desperation to know what was in those envelopes.

After loosely sifting through the contents, the Spanish officer shut the briefcase and held it out to the British man. "You'll be wanting this back, no doubt."

Sera looked at the two of them, wondering what would happen next. Of course he should take the briefcase. It came from a British soldier and should be returned to one, especially if it contained top secret information. The British officer's eyes widened, as if he wasn't sure what to say. Only a bumbling fool would refuse to take his country's top secret information back, but if he did, Mincemeat Man was finished.

The British officer decided to play the role of bumbling fool. "Well, your superior might not like that," he finally said. "So perhaps you should deliver it to him, and then bring it back to me, following the official route."

The Spanish officer only shrugged, gathered up the items that had been in Martin's pockets, and left. The American followed. His face had gotten greener and greener with the smell, and once outside, he'd probably run for the nearest bush.

With that, the doctor requested tools to begin the autopsy. Sera pressed in closer and reminded herself *again* that she was here not only as a scientist, but also as a spy. And spies could not get sick, no matter how disgusting this was.

But when he cut into the body, her understanding of gross went to an entirely new level. The insides were rotted and watery. Sera knew how long this body had been frozen, and how far the body would decompose in that time. But she couldn't let the doctor think it had been more than a few days.

"So much decomposition?" he wondered aloud. "Strange."

"Maybe it's the seawater," Sera offered. If Martin had drowned at sea, the doctor would expect to find seawater in his lungs. And seawater was hard on a human body. "The seawater and the heat," she added.

"And the skin is quite discolored," he said.

"Probably the effects from lack of air underwater," Sera said. It wasn't that. The man had actually died from eating rat poison, which contained high levels of phosphorous. That's what had turned his skin yellow. But she hoped the doctor wouldn't think too long or hard about it.

To her, the signs that Martin hadn't died at sea were so obvious. But the doctor had no reason to suspect it was anything else, so she hoped he'd keep trying to find ways to explain Martin's condition that were consistent for a drowning.

Finally, the doctor wiped his brow with the back

of his arm. "It's quite warm for an autopsy, don't you agree?"

"The smell is . . . a bit much," the British officer replied.

"To be thorough, I need more time."

The doctor wasn't stupid, and that worried Sera. With more time, he was bound to realize Martin had been dead long before he was dumped into the sea. And if he figured that out, word would get back to the Nazis no matter what Sera told Clauss. She spoke quickly. "Of course, this heat will continue to degrade the body, even worse than what's already happened since he was pulled ashore. Very soon, it will be hard to know anything for sure."

"True. You are a bright girl." The doctor pursed his lips, then ordered his assistant to help him move the body into a wood coffin behind them. "Let the death certificate state that this is a drowning victim, in the water for eight to ten days."

"Very good," the British officer said, probably too quickly. He must know about the plan, Sera thought, or at least, enough to know his role in this morgue today.

Before the lid went on, the doctor placed a hand on the coffin. "Still, there are questions that should be answered. A drowning victim is always, er, nibbled on by the fish. I see none of that here. Seawater should have made his hair brittle and stiff. But it is not. Even his clothes are in better condition than I would have expected for a man floating this long in the water."

As if sensing she was on his side, the British officer locked eyes with Sera. She looked up at the doctor. "These are good questions. I'm sure you'll want others to come and check your work. The Germans, perhaps."

The doctor frowned down at her. No, he didn't want the Germans checking his work any more than he wanted to be hung upside down and subjected to tickle torture. "It is death by drowning," the doctor said firmly. "That is my final conclusion. His body will be returned immediately to the British for burial."

Sera nodded and recorded his findings on her clipboard, but inside she was beaming. Operation Fix Mincemeat Man had just cleared its first hurdle.

Riq's Choice

THE FOLLOWING day, after Riq had finished his assigned work, he ate his lunch near a telegraph machine so he could watch the messages being sent from Britain to various government officials in Spain. He only saw a few of them, but he could tell how carefully worded the messages were. They had to sound eager to get the body back, but not too eager. And of course, they couldn't actually get the body back until Spain had control of the documents. Everyone who seemed to know about the plan was playing it cool, but he knew better. If this went badly, the Allies wouldn't recover during this war. Or ever recover, for that matter.

But that night at nine o'clock, he settled in near the pay phone, waiting for calls from Dak and Sera. Riq stared harder at the phone as if that would somehow make it ring. He hadn't heard from either of them their first night apart, but he hoped to hear something soon.

Sera's part of the plan was crucial and he was going crazy wondering if she'd had any luck. Even worse was knowing that Dak was somewhere behind enemy lines.

Finally, the phone rang once and stopped. After a few seconds, it rang again. That was the signal. It was either Dak or Sera calling him.

Footsteps echoed on the quiet street behind him and Riq kept his head down. There were many officers in this area and he didn't need to get their attention now. All he wanted was to answer the phone.

"You there," a man said, addressing Riq. "Why are you out so late? Causing trouble?"

"No, sir," Riq answered.

"That's too bad," a woman's voice said. "Because we are."

Even before he turned around, Riq knew who had come. That was Tilda's voice, cold and harsh. She made porcupines seem cuddly. Riq's legs turned to mush, and he had to force himself to turn. Tilda stood between two sloppy and unshaven men who were roughly the size of small mountains. Aside from their British uniforms, they looked nothing like soldiers. Although he couldn't see weapons in their hands, he didn't doubt for a minute that they had them.

"Answer that phone," Tilda ordered. "It's for you, right?"

Riq had almost forgotten it was still ringing, and couldn't understand why the caller hadn't given up already. Maybe they were in trouble, or needed help. But as he stared into the black eyes of Tilda and her friends, Riq began to think nobody needed more help at the moment than him.

"Pick up the phone," Tilda repeated. "And if you say anything I don't like, you're going to regret it."

Riq picked up the phone and, instantly, Tilda was in the phone box at his side, her ear pressed to the outside of the receiver for whatever she could hear.

"Riq!" Dak's voice came through with a lot of static and sounded far away. "Riq, is that you?"

"Y-yes," Riq stammered.

"What took you so long to answer? Were you napping while Sera and I had the dangerous jobs?"

Riq gritted his teeth. Sometimes he really hated that kid. "I've got problems here, too, you know."

"Well, unless your problem is that wicked witch of the future, it's not worse than mine," Dak said, unknowingly earning Riq a jab in the ribs with Tilda's pointy elbow. "You won't believe where I am."

"I'm sure I won't," Riq said. "So there's really no reason to tell me." He bit into his last words as Tilda kicked him in the shin.

Beside him, Tilda motioned that Riq should keep Dak talking. Maybe she didn't know that kid never needed any encouragement to run his mouth.

"Are you okay?" Dak asked. "You sound—"

"Tired," Riq finished. "And I bet you are, too, since you had to travel all the way to Switzerland today."

"What? No, I'm not in Switzerland. You know I went to—"

"Quietville." If Dak couldn't catch the subtle cues, Riq would try a more obvious one. "You're at the Keep Your Mouth Closed for Once Hotel."

"Hitler's headquarters in Berlin. They gave me a job—oh!" Then Dak realized what Riq had just said. "Oh, uh, I mean—"

Finally, it seemed that Tilda had heard enough. She ducked out of the phone box and motioned at her thugs, who grabbed Riq's arms and ripped him away from the phone. One of them clamped a hand over his mouth while the other pulled his arms behind his back and held them there.

"Hello?" Dak's voice could be heard coming from the receiver, dangling by its cord. "Hel-lo!"

Tilda returned to the booth, picked up the phone, and glared at Riq for a moment before she spoke into the receiver. "You know my voice, don't you, Dak?" Her oily grin widened. "Good. Now, do you want your friend to die?"

It would be okay if I did, Riq thought, and he hoped Dak would refuse to bargain for his life. Riq knew he was running out of his own time line pretty fast—and missing the last few slides through history wouldn't make that much of a difference.

But Dak must've answered no, because Tilda's smirk widened again and she said, "Then you will tell me where the Infinity Ring is."

Riq tried to yell out for Dak not to say anything, but the hand was still covering his mouth. He sat helplessly as Tilda listened to whatever Dak said.

"You have the time-travel device?" Tilda's tone was doubtful. "An object that could literally hand control of the entire world to Adolf Hitler, and you brought it with you to Germany?"

Whatever Dak said in answer, Tilda wasn't buying it. "I think you're lying," she said. "I think you're trying to protect your friends. Who has it, Riq or Sera?"

Riq heard Dak protesting when Tilda pulled the phone away from her ear, but her eyes only narrowed in on his. "You remember my friend Anton, correct? He spies on the British when needed, and spies on the Germans equally well."

A triple spy, Riq thought. One who had access to both sides of the war, but was loyal only to the SQ.

Tilda added, "Anton and another of our agents, Cleo, have access to that same headquarters. I expect Anton has made his way back to Germany by now."

Riq's teeth were clenched so tightly together that he could barely speak. "So?"

"I want you to tell me if Dak has the Infinity Ring. Because if he does, then my next call will be to Anton and Cleo. By tomorrow morning, Dak will be nothing but a distant memory. So, tell me, Riq, does Dak have the Infinity Ring?"

Riq closed his eyes to think. Dak didn't have the

Infinity Ring, so nothing was really gained by lying to Tilda. And he couldn't let her make that call to Berlin and endanger Dak. But what could he possibly say to buy them all some more time?

He shook his head and then opened his eyes. "Dak doesn't have the Ring."

"Then who does?"

Riq tried to keep his voice even and to look straight at Tilda. "None of us have it. The Hystorian of this time period has it."

"Nonsense," Tilda said. "The only Hystorian in this area was killed in an air raid in Aberdeen." She smiled evilly. "I'm from the future, too, remember? You've lost your one advantage." She held the phone back up to her ear and said, "Listen carefully, Dak, because even though you just tried lying to me, what I'm about to tell you is the exact truth. I've got Riq, and if you do not tell me where the Ring is this moment, you will never see him alive again."

There was a long silence while Riq strained to hear Dak's response on the phone. But he couldn't hear anything and only knew Dak had answered when Tilda hung up the phone and turned to her thugs. "The girl has it and she's somewhere in Spain. We need to know exactly where she is."

"This kid can tell us."

Riq shook his head. "I don't know," he said. "She typed in the coordinates, and I don't know them."

"Will she call?" Tilda asked. Without Riq's help, she answered her own question. "Of course she will. We just have to be patient and wait for her to get in touch."

"What about him?" one of the thugs asked, gesturing at Riq.

"We have to keep him alive, for now," Tilda said. "We might still need his help to get that Ring."

It was a bad situation. All right, Riq admitted to himself, it was a *terrible* situation, but at least Dak was safe, and with any luck he might even find some way to warn Sera.

Or, that was what he thought before Tilda picked up the telephone once more and started dialing.

"Who are you calling now?" the other thug asked.

"Anton and Cleo, our friends in Berlin," Tilda said. "Maybe we still need Riq alive, but we don't need Dak."

Dodging the SQ

Dak was in a full-blown panic by the time Tilda hung up on him. She had Riq, and who knew what she'd do to him if things didn't go her way? She also knew that Sera had the Infinity Ring. The only reason he didn't wonder if things could get any worse is because he already knew the answer: Even now, things could always get worse.

He needed to help both Sera and Riq, but didn't have a single idea for how to begin. Obviously, it wouldn't do any good to call Riq back, and he had no way to contact Sera, or any money to get from Berlin all the way to Spain.

Dak returned to the kitchen and slumped against a wall while he tried to force himself to keep thinking. He had to calm down, because if he panicked any worse, he'd do something crazy like rip off all his clothes and start running in circles, screaming.

Riq was in the most immediate danger. But Tilda would probably keep him alive until she had the

Infinity Ring. Riq was smart and strong, and likely had a trick or two up his sleeve. If there was any chance to escape, Riq would find it. And then Riq could warn Sera.

Dak forced his fists to unclench. That wasn't much to base his hope on, but it was better than nothing. For now, the only thing Dak could do was to try to wedge his way closer to Hitler and make sure that once the fake plans from Mincemeat came through, Hitler would believe them.

Dak half-smiled. *Yeah, just as easy as mincemeat pie.*

Except that there were a few complications. First, Hitler only took advice from the small group of people he trusted. That group didn't include Dak. Second, only a few people ever got close to Hitler at all, and as far as Dak knew, none of them were eleven years old. And third, if Dak ever did get close to Hitler, he could never pretend to be on Hitler's side long enough to convince him of anything. The man was too evil, too cruel. Dak knew *that* much pretending just wasn't in him.

At some point, Dak must've fallen asleep against the wall because he awoke to the sound of a man and woman in the hallway just outside the kitchen. Even through the walls, he recognized Anton's voice. But it now bore a German accent.

"Tilda said the boy was here!" At that, Dak's eyes sprung fully open. Instantly, he was wide awake. Wide awake and trapped.

"You know the Führer would not want us roaming around at night," a woman's voice said. "We can look for the boy in the morning."

At one point while he had been on the phone with Tilda, Dak had thought he heard her threaten to send SQ agents after him here in Berlin. But the static had been so thick on the phone, he had hoped he heard wrong. Apparently not. He looked around for a place to hide, but where was he supposed to go? A cupboard?

"Who are you more afraid of?" Anton asked. "Tilda or the Führer?"

Dak asked himself the same question. It was sort of like asking which was the better way to die: by lightning or by getting thrown off a cliff. Neither option sounded particularly fun, and both ended the same way.

"She said that if we don't catch him, this boy could destroy the SQ." Anton paused while some closets were opened, searched, and shut again. "Maybe we shouldn't do this. Back at the Admiralty, one of the kids – the girl – told me she had been to the future, and that everything gets destroyed. I'm worried, Cleo. What if we're wrong?"

Cleo scoffed at that. "Do you trust three kids more than Tilda, one of our own? She said she can stop the Cataclysm and I believe her. And if we help her, she will reward us well once she's in control. Now let's find the boy, and then go after the others."

"And if the Führer catches us, he will say we are spying against him and have us arrested!" In his nervousness, Anton's voice was just a touch too loud.

"Be quiet, or we *will* be caught," Cleo said. "Let's check the kitchen. If he's not there, we can resume the search tomorrow."

The kitchen. Where he was. Just his luck. They could've chosen any of a dozen rooms to search, but of course they chose the one place he was.

Dak darted one direction and then the next, hoping a good hiding spot would pop out at him. But it was too late, and the kitchen door was already opening. So he ducked behind a cabinet and folded himself into the smallest ball he could make. And waited to be caught. From a certain angle, he would be all too visible.

"He won't be in here," Anton said. "If he was allowed to spend the night in these headquarters, they'd have given him a bed."

"But I think this time traveler will be awake tonight," Cleo answered. "He'll be snooping around the place."

Awake, yes. But snooping around a bunker loaded with Nazis? No. Dak considered himself brave, but not stupid.

"Check the back of the room," Cleo ordered. "I'll look over here."

The back of the room. Dak figured the only thing that could've made him more obvious back here was if a large blinking arrow somehow lit up over his head. He could see Cleo's reflection in a metal cabinet between them. She wasn't much taller than him but was built like a wrestler. Her dark hair was pulled back into a neat bun and her face was pinched with irritation.

"Be ready for when we find him," Cleo said. "When you see him, just do it fast."

Dak understood those words. They wouldn't question him, or give him a warning. There would be no chances for escape and no one would come to rescue him here. They wanted him dead and nothing else.

But then the door opened and a new voice said, "You two, what are you doing up so late?"

The tension in the room shot up so quickly, Dak could actually feel the change in the air.

"Colonel Von Roenne, we were just searching for a—a, uh, lost ring," Cleo said.

Von Roenne? Dak had heard the name before, but couldn't quite place it. He reassured himself that if he were not on the brink of being captured, tortured, and likely killed either by the SQ or by the Nazis, that he could probably remember who Colonel Von Roenne had been.

"Whose ring?" Von Roenne surveyed the room until his gaze fell directly on Dak, who quickly waved his hands, silently begging the German not to reveal him. He knew that he must've looked scared and alone, but Dak didn't care if he did. He *was* scared and alone.

Von Roenne turned back to Cleo. "You can find

your ring in the morning. Until then, the Führer does not want people wandering the halls at all hours of the night. Now go!"

"Yes, Colonel," Anton said, hastily sweeping both himself and Cleo out the door.

Once they had gone, Von Roenne impatiently said, "Well? Come out, boy."

Dak poked his head up over the counter to find Von Roenne staring back at him, arms folded. He was a thin man whose short, neatly combed hair revealed a deep widow's peak, and he wore round glasses that gave him a strict, studious look. He didn't seem to be the type of person who smiled often, but then, his voice was also gentler than Dak had expected from a high-ranking Nazi. At least Von Roenne had sent the SQ duo away. Dak figured his odds of surviving the next few minutes were pretty even.

"I haven't seen you before," Von Roenne said to Dak.

Dak said nothing. Mostly because he was sure if he tried speaking, it would come out in some high-pitched squeal of terror that'd wake the entire house.

"Can you tell me why those two were looking for you?" Von Roenne asked. "What might two Nazis want with a young boy working in the kitchen?"

Okay, maybe he wouldn't scream, but he was also pretty sure his mouth had forgotten how to form actual words. So Dak only shrugged his shoulders and hoped the end would come quickly and painlessly.

"I think you must have played a joke on them and gotten caught," Von Roenne said. "Yes?"

Well, yes. *If* the joke was getting himself inside the most dangerous place in Germany.

Then Von Roenne smiled, just a little. "I suppose I played a joke or two myself when I was younger. But these are not the kind of people you want to tease."

"No, sir," Dak mumbled. Frankly, he was already pretty clear on that fact.

"And remember that you now owe me a favor in return. Do not forget."

Dak nodded. If there was one thing he would never forget, it was what Von Roenne had just done for him.

"Now, let's have no more trouble," Von Roenne said. "Something has been found in Spain, something that might give us a great advantage over the Allies, and there is tension in the bunker. You'll be smart to stay out of everyone's way."

"Yes, sir," Dak mumbled.

Von Roenne nodded at him, then left the kitchen. Once he'd gone, Dak slumped back down to the ground, exhausted, and never so scared in his life.

Sera's Warnings

SERA HAD intended to call Riq that first evening. She felt desperate to know how he was, and whether Dak had made it to Germany safely. But she had the chilling feeling somebody was watching her, most likely that creepy Clauss. It wasn't worth the risk to make a phone call.

She did, however, discover a surprising fact that made her want to call Riq even more. One of their first adventures had been on board Christopher Columbus's ship as it sailed for the new world. This Spanish city, Huelva, had looked familiar to her from the start, but it was only after she began wandering the busy port town that she realized why. Four hundred and fifty years had changed a lot of things, but not the basic landscape. She was now less than ten miles from where she, Dak, and Riq had boarded Columbus's ship. For such a small coastal lagoon in the big world, it had seen its share of history. Dak would completely geek out about that. But not tonight, not until she was sure it was safe to call.

In the meantime, she had to live the life of a spy. And that meant lying, something that Sera wasn't altogether comfortable with. It was one thing to lie to Clauss, but the doctor seemed like a good man, and Sera took no pleasure in deceiving him. She'd managed to convince him that she'd come to town from an impoverished village in order to pursue her love of science, something her family didn't understand. He allowed her to stay the night in a small room above his garage—but warned her that he would be putting her on the next bus out of town. "A girl's place is with her family," he had said.

Sera hadn't had to fake the lump in her throat at hearing that. Until then, she had managed to avoid thinking about how her parents had been SQ. But now she felt torn. Her mind struggled to understand how they could have aligned themselves with such evil people. And her heart longed for an explanation that would make everything okay. Despite everything, she still wanted to see them again.

Sera spent the following day hoping to bump into Clauss, but he was nowhere to be found. The day after that was a funeral for Major Martin attended by the same British officer who had been at the postmortem, some disinterested Spanish officers, and a few curious people from the town. Even if she hadn't been there on spy duty, Sera wanted to attend the ceremony. She might've been the only person there who knew Major

Martin was really a homeless man who'd died a few months ago from eating rat poison. He may not have given his life for his country, but he had given his death. For that, he deserved to be honored.

A couple of times during the funeral, she saw the top of Clauss's crisp blond hair poking into people's whispered conversations as if eavesdropping for anything suspicious. Perhaps he was hoping Martin's briefcase might somehow fall from the sky and land in his lap. But it wasn't until the guests left that he found her, sitting on a bench near the cemetery. Just to have him beside her felt like a cold wind had blown in. But she kept her calm.

"I heard a rumor that Major Martin drowned at sea," he said. "Probably after his plane crashed."

"That's what the doctor decided."

"Why didn't any other bodies wash up on shore? Where's the plane wreckage?"

Don't appear too obvious, Sera reminded herself. If she was supposed to be on Germany's side, then she should be hopeful, but not yet convinced.

"That's a good point," she said. "You should probably wait another week or two and see if anything else washes up."

"Stupid girl!" Clauss crossed his legs and turned away from her. "If Martin was carrying information, we can't wait two weeks to get it."

Sera tried to hide her smile. That's what she'd hoped he'd think. Who was stupid now?

"Martin had papers with him, correct? In a briefcase?"

Sera nodded. She wanted to tell him the entire fake plan, to convince him right then that Martin was real, that Britain was invading Greece and not Sicily, and that he should tell Hitler just to surrender now. But the truth was that she hadn't seen anything written on the papers. Right now, it was more important to make Clauss trust *her*. And to get that trust, she had to tell him the truth.

"He had papers," she said. "But I couldn't see what they said. There were envelopes inside the briefcase, too, and they were sealed." Then, just in case it helped, she added, "The British officer in the room didn't seem very happy that Spain has them."

Clauss smiled. "That's because many officials in Spain quietly support Germany in this war. But they can't just hand the papers over to us. Our work must be . . . subtler." He stood and withdrew from his pocket a single coin. "That's for your trouble."

"Only one?" Sera said. "This won't buy anything."

"Then find me more information," Clauss said.

Sera nodded and he left. Only then did her heart begin to beat normally again. Had she done enough? Would the papers really make their way into German hands without any further effort on her part?

She was so lost in thought that she didn't realize the doctor was approaching her until he sat on the bench where Clauss had just been. "Sera, why were you speaking with that man?" he asked.

"Clauss?" Sera tried to keep her cool, but her heart rate was already back up again. "He was curious about Major Martin. He wanted to know what happened to the briefcase. I . . ." She decided to go for it. "I told him I was curious about that, too. Do you know what the man who took it will do with it?"

The doctor scowled. "He will keep it under lock and key until he's ordered to take it to his superiors in Madrid. It's none of my business, and if you're smart, you'll leave it alone, too."

"But—"

The doctor grabbed her shoulders and nearly shook her. "Right now, Martin's papers are at the center of a world war. If you meddle, you will get in the way of some very dangerous people." He released her and then pulled some money from his pocket, which he shoved into her hands. "Clauss isn't fooling anyone. He's almost certainly spying for Berlin. If you need money, it isn't worth making a devil's bargain with him. Take this instead. Use it to leave town, return to your family while you can. The Nazi spies will know you saw those papers. I never should have allowed you in that room. I wish *I* had not been in that room!"

Sera pocketed the money and thanked him, promising she would consider what he'd said. Then she made her way back into town. The worry in the doctor's voice bothered her more than she wanted to admit. Obviously, she knew this was dangerous, but hadn't she been playing a dangerous game since the moment she and Dak stumbled into time travel? What made anything different now?

Sera knew the answer. On past missions, she had Riq with her, or Dak, or both of them. Now they were all separated, all fighting their individual battles, and she felt totally cut off from even knowing whether both boys were still okay.

Focus, Sera told herself. Focus on the job that had to be done. For now, that was the most important thing.

So she went back to hunting for any information that might be useful to Clauss. She hoped to hear some gossip or rumors about what was happening to Martin's papers, but if anyone had something worth sharing, they didn't let her in on the conversation. It was strange to be in the spy business, pretending to want one thing when she really wanted the very opposite. It was exhausting, actually.

The following evening, Sera decided to take the risk and call Riq. It had been five days since she'd arrived in Spain, and she hadn't dared make a phone call. But she couldn't go without hearing news any longer.

She found a pay phone not far from a fruit stand and dialed the number Riq had given her. She let it ring once, then hung up, then retrieved her coin and dialed again. It rang only once before someone picked up.

"Hello?" Riq asked.

Sera was so happy to hear a friendly voice, her words

came out in an explosion of information. She told him about the postmortem examination, Clauss, and even Columbus's ship. Finally, she drew in a breath long enough to hear him telling her to stop talking. "Why?" she asked. "What's wrong? Is Dak okay? Are you?"

Now that she was listening, Riq's voice was clearly strained. "Do you still have the Infinity Ring?" he asked.

"Yes, of course. Why?"

"You need to leave Spain. Go anywhere. Get—" Then his words ended in a groan and the phone went silent.

"Riq!" Sera yelled. "Riq!"

Someone on the other end of the line picked up the phone. She heard breathing before any words were spoken. Then someone whispered, "Sera." The voice was like she imagined a snake would sound. "Sera, do you know who I am?"

"Tilda." Sera's hand began shaking so hard she almost dropped the phone.

"If you leave the country with that Infinity Ring, what do you think will happen to Riq?"

"Leave him alone!"

"Tomorrow, Riq and I will be in Madrid, the capital of Spain. If you want him back, then meet me in Retiro Park at noon with the Infinity Ring. Beside the lake is a large monument. Be there, or you will never see Riq again."

Sera started to answer but the line went dead. She hung up her phone and clutched the sack holding the

Infinity Ring in her hands. What was she supposed to do now?

There wasn't time for her to answer her own question. Only seconds after she left the phone booth, Clauss appeared and gripped her arm so tightly it made her wince. He dug into her pocket and pulled out the money from the doctor.

"Who gave you this?"

"The doctor at the morgue."

"And who were you talking to just now?"

Sera tried to break free, but it did no good. "A friend of mine who's coming to Madrid. I have to go see him. Now let me go!"

"Madrid?" Clauss released her arm but stepped closer to her. "You don't have enough money to get there."

No, she didn't. And she couldn't use the Infinity Ring again, not so soon. There had to be another way.

"I'm trying to get you more information," Sera said. "You could pay me now, and then —"

"I have a better plan." Clauss withdrew an envelope from his suit jacket and held it out to her. "If you safely deliver this letter for me, I will help you get to Madrid."

"Deliver the letter to who?" Sera figured she was already in enough trouble, and so was Riq. Mincemeat Man would have to wait until she knew what to do about Tilda.

Clauss sighed. "I tried everything I could think of to get Major Martin's papers these past few days. No matter what I try, the officials here are protecting them far too well. So well, in fact, that I am sure they must contain some important information."

Very important, Sera thought. So important that it was driving her crazy. Spain was supposed to hand the papers over to the Nazis, not protect them!

Clauss continued, "Martin's briefcase is being sent to Madrid today. It is very embarrassing to me to lose access to it, and the Führer will be disappointed in my failures. This letter is for my friend in Madrid. It explains why I could not get the briefcase and hopefully he can explain to the Führer."

"Why not just mail it, or deliver it yourself?" Sera asked.

"Letters such as these do not go through the mail, and this town is my post. I'm not allowed to leave."

Sera folded her arms and stared up at him. "So you'll pay my way to Madrid, and then trust me to carry that letter there?"

Clauss shook his head. "I don't trust anyone. But I also know that if there's any trouble along the way, the Allies will never search a young girl. And if you fail to deliver this letter, or if you open it yourself, my friend in Madrid will find you, and please believe me when I say that he is more desperate and far less kind than I am."

Sera reached for the letter but saw nothing written for the address. "Who is it for?"

"Major Karl-Erich Kuhlenthal. He is one of Hitler's most trusted men in Spain, or he once was. If he doesn't get Martin's papers, then his career is finished."

"What does he think about Major Martin?"

Clauss shrugged. "If Kuhlenthal can get the papers, and if they're real, then he will save his career. So for his sake, I hope they are real."

For safekeeping, Sera stuffed the letter in the bag holding the Infinity Ring. Before dropping her off at the train station, Clauss even bought her a small suitcase to help her look more like a traveler, then put her on a train to Madrid.

"Major Kuhlenthal should meet you at the train station, but if he doesn't, then you can always find him at the Spanish Ministry. Give him this letter, and then stay out of his way if you want to be safe."

Sera nodded, and ran his words through her mind as the train pulled away from the station. She would give Kuhlenthal the letter, and she definitely wanted to be safe. But if Mincemeat Man was going to succeed, the last thing she could do was stay out of his way.

14

In Tilda's Grip

SERA ARRIVED at the Madrid train station early the next morning. The air was cool, but the skies were clear. Hopefully, it would warm up before she turned into a PopSQicle.

She had the letter for Major Kuhlenthal clutched in her hand. For most of the train ride, that's where it had been, so she would be sure not to lose it. The ride here had been crowded and miserable, with people speaking so many languages that it drove the translator in her ear nuts. At one point she had been pushed into a small kitchen area where she was nearly burned by a hot coffeepot. For a few moments she stared at it as she considered using it to steam open the envelope. Then she could know what the letter said. However, Dak had once told her about an old spy trick of leaving something inconspicuous in the seal of an envelope, such as an eyelash or hair, to test whether someone else had opened it. She wondered if Clauss had done that to the letter for Major Kuhlenthal, or for that matter, whether the British had done that with Major Martin's sealed letters.

Clauss hadn't been clear on where she was supposed to meet Kuhlenthal, only that he would meet her at the train station. And that question was answered the instant she stepped off the train.

The tall man standing on the train platform immediately reminded her of a hawk. His sharp blue eyes were on her the moment she emerged, and the weight of his glare made her feet drag as she shuffled forward. He looked her over like he was examining a moldy piece of bread.

"You're the child sent by Clauss?" he asked.

Sera tried not to let her irritation show. "Yes."

"What does it say about the Nazis that we need the help of a young girl?"

Sera had more than a few ideas of what she'd say about the Nazis, but she only straightened up tall and said, "I saw the postmortem and the papers inside the briefcase. Nobody would suspect someone like me."

"I hope he didn't pay you too much for that useless information," Kuhlenthal said. "Those papers are probably fakes anyway. We are suspicious."

"It's good that you are," Sera said. "Because I think Captain Clauss believes they're real. You should let him write to the Führer about the papers. If he's wrong, he'll get the blame."

"And if he's right, he'll get the credit!" Kuhlenthal shook his head sharply. "No. If the Führer is going to reward one of his officers, it must be me."

Sera glanced at a clock on the wall of the station. She wasn't sure how long it would take for her to get to Retiro Park from here, but she didn't see the point of sticking around just to get insulted again.

"Listen, I've got to go," Sera said. "If you don't need my help—"

"I don't," Kuhlenthal said. "Not unless you can read English well. I speak the language, but once I get those papers, it might help to have another set of eyes on them."

Sera smiled. "I read it as well as if I'd grown up with it." She eyed the clock again. "I'd really better go, but I'll try to stay close to the Ministry. If you need to find me, that's where I'll be."

Kuhlenthal dismissed her, but she felt his attention still on her as she ran off. Hopefully, she could shake off his eyes in time to take care of some quick business at the train station and then make the exchange with Tilda.

With so many other passengers getting off in Madrid, it took Sera some time to locate a taxi to take her to the park, and it cost her all the money the doctor had given her a few days earlier. She was getting hungry, and the food from the markets she passed only made the hunger worse, but nothing could be done about that.

Once she arrived at Retiro Park, Sera took time to become familiar with the area and gather a few things in preparation for meeting Tilda. Then she found a quiet hiding place by the lake where she could see everyone who came and went. While she waited, it was hard not to get distracted by the majesty of the park. A series of Roman columns arched around an open gathering place. In the center of it, overlooking the lake, was a huge marble monument with several statues surrounding it. The largest statue on top was done in bronze, and was a tribute to a former Spanish king astride his horse.

At exactly twelve o'clock, Tilda whisked right past Sera's hiding place, strode through the marble columns, and stood impatiently beside the monument. Sera watched her for a few minutes, checking whether she was there alone, and whether enough people were around that she could call for help if needed. But where was Riq? Did Tilda really expect to get the Infinity Ring without Riq there to trade?

Of course she did. Tilda was controlling this exchange. To save Riq, Tilda expected Sera to do anything Tilda demanded.

Sera emerged from her hiding place with the suitcase Clauss had given her in both hands. She passed through the marble columns and caught Tilda's eye.

Tilda didn't smile, didn't even flinch a muscle. She simply stood as expressionless as the statue above her.

"There's no point in you taking the Infinity Ring," Sera said. "I'm the only one who can operate it because it works off my DNA."

"Let me worry about that."

Tilda reached for the suitcase, but Sera clutched it to her chest and locked her arms around it.

Tilda reached out a spiny hand and plucked a hair from Sera's head, then folded it into her palm. "Problem solved."

Sera gritted her teeth. She should've seen that one coming. "You still don't get the Ring until I get Riq back."

"And you don't get to set the terms here!" Tilda's eyes darted around as other people took notice of their conversation. Lowering her voice, she said, "Hand that over, and I'll tell you where to find your friend."

"Maybe I've changed my mind." Sera back stepped away from Tilda. "You just want the Ring so you can control time, but that doesn't work! The fabric of reality can't take that kind of abuse. All you can do is make your own place in history."

Tilda grabbed the suitcase. "Oh, that's exactly what I plan to do. Trust me."

Sera tugged back, but Tilda had a strong hold on it. "You won't be able to figure it out!" Sera said.

"Then maybe you should come and help me." By

then Tilda had the suitcase handle in one hand, and the other locked around Sera's arm. Sera tried pulling away, but Tilda wasn't giving in. And for Sera's plan to work, she *had* to give this creep the slip.

She had come to save Riq, but now it looked as if she was going to be captured right along with him!

Riq's Escape

RIQ AWOKE in darkness with the back of his head feeling like someone was hitting it with a mallet. He raised his hands to calm the headache, then realized they were tied in front of him. His legs were tied, too, and he must have been this way for some time because his lower leg had fallen asleep and was tingling with pain.

Riq tried to shake it out, but the jostling only made his arm brush along something beneath him that was sharp and left small cuts in his skin. Where was he anyway?

Wiggling his body around, Riq felt a low metal roof over his head, an uneven floor, and metal sides. Then he groaned. This was the trunk of a car. An early model SQuautomobile, no doubt.

The last thing he remembered was being on the phone with Sera, trying to warn her about Tilda. Then someone clunked him on the head and now he was in here. The car was stopped, which might mean they had already arrived wherever they were going. Probably Spain, where Sera and the Infinity Ring were.

Riq rolled again, hoping to find a way out of the trunk. He couldn't kick his way free; even feeling the thick metal with his hands he could tell it was far more solid than the cars of his era. Maybe it was true what his grandmother had always told him. Maybe things *were* made better back in the day.

So he moved to his back again, but this time he landed directly on that sharp edge of metal. He wasn't sure exactly what it was, but it was hard to avoid and would have him in slices by the time someone came for him. He tried shifting, but the ropes around his wrists got caught on the metal piece.

Riq rolled his eyes—it was one of his biggest "duh" moments ever. Immediately, he started scraping the rope against the metal, letting the sharp edge dig deeper and deeper into the fibers. It took him longer than he wanted, but finally there was a snap and the rope loosened. He shook it off, then crouched forward and began untying the rope around his feet.

Once he was free, he felt around the trunk for any way to release the latch, but nothing he pressed on did any good, and there didn't seem to be anything with him in this trunk that could be used to escape. His only choice was to wait until someone opened the trunk from the outside. Maybe if he jumped up at just the right time . . .

Maybe not. Tilda's two SQ thugs were big guys, and unless they were half asleep they'd catch him before he even got to a sitting position.

And it might already be too late. The car had been parked for some time. Tilda might have the Ring now. She was desperate to get it; she had talked about nothing else while she had him captured, waiting each night for Sera to call. She kept asking Riq about it until he convinced her that only Sera knew how to operate it or how it worked.

But then he heard the car doors open and shut, and voices outside the trunk — the two SQ men. They were arguing about something, though he couldn't catch any of the words. Then one man yelled to the other to stop talking so loudly or Tilda would be furious with them, and Riq couldn't help but smile. No matter how big and brutal those guys were, they were still afraid of Tilda.

When the trunk lid opened, Riq was lying on his side in the same position as when he'd first awoken. The ropes were over his wrists and ankles as if he was still tied up, and his eyes were closed.

"How hard did you hit him anyway?" one of the men asked.

"I dunno. Is he still alive?"

The first guy reached down and felt for the pulse at his neck. "Of course he is. And what do we care if he's hurt anyway? Once we have the Infinity Ring, it doesn't matter if he lives."

Riq resented that. It mattered a great deal to him whether he lived.

"All I care about is the money she promised us. Nothing else."

"What does money matter?" The man speaking now lowered his voice to almost a whisper. "If we stay close to Tilda until she has the Ring, *we* could take it for ourselves and sell it for all the money in the world."

They both laughed greedily. Then one of them asked, "Do you think that girl is at the lake yet?"

"How would I know? But Tilda left a long time ago. We need to make room in this trunk. When she gets the Ring, she'll bring the girl back here. Then we'll take them both for a long ride. Maybe Tilda, too."

"A long, one-way ride," the other man said, chuckling. He reached forward to scoot Riq's body deeper into the trunk. When he did, Riq shot out his legs and kicked the man backward. Soccer practice had been useful for something other than making goals. It also built excellent leg muscles.

The man stumbled back, knocking the other to the ground with him, and Riq leapt from the trunk like a cannon had shot him out of there. Both men got to their feet and began chasing him down the street.

The car had been parked in a sort of alley but across from a large park – probably the park where Sera was supposed to meet Tilda. The thugs said they weren't sure if that meeting had happened yet, only that it would happen near a lake.

But it couldn't be just anywhere at the lake. There would have to be some sort of landmark. Someplace easy for both of them to find. He had to look for something like that.

He ran across the street with the two SQ men not far behind him. But again, soccer was paying off. Riq could run fast, and he was sure they would get tired before he did. The park was busy today, and Riq did his best to not get tangled in the crowds. He passed a small fountain and paused to look back, but saw the SQ men just on the opposite side. One lunged for him and ended up splashing into the fountain.

Up ahead was a group of children, probably on a school trip. Riq weaved among them effortlessly and then darted off the trail at an intersection, onto a small path between tall rows of thick green shrubs. He squeezed between two shrubs and used a tiny hole in the greenery to peek through.

The men caught up to the schoolchildren, which slowed them down considerably. They came to the intersection and looked in all directions, then continued down the main park trail. Riq exhaled in relief. At least for now, he was safe.

But he couldn't stay hidden. He had to find Sera, and fast.

Riq emerged from his hiding place and saw a man and his wife not far from him. He tapped the man's shoulder, then in Spanish asked him if there were any landmarks near the lake. The man rolled his eyes as if Riq had just asked the most obvious question in the world, right up there with which direction he should look to find the sky. But he told him to look for the great monument, jerked a finger in that direction, and Riq went running, tossing a *gracias* behind him.

Riq soon found the lake, but it was a long way around to the other side, where a tall bronze statue portrayed a man on a horse surrounded by smaller white columns. Steps led from the statue down to the water and, in the center of them all, was Tilda, perfectly straight and still, waiting for Sera.

Riq looked around him again. The thugs were here somewhere, knowing this was where he'd go. But where were they?

Then he saw another figure emerge onto the steps. Sera. In her hands was some sort of suitcase. She must've put the Infinity Ring in there for safety. She clutched it to her chest, unwilling to give it up, and then she spoke to Tilda for a moment.

Riq began running. As fast as he could and with no care for whether the men would jump out at him. Sera could not give up that Ring, and she definitely could not go anywhere with Tilda.

He called out Sera's name but a breeze was blowing in his face, carrying his words away from the stone steps. He waved his arms, hoping to make Sera see him, desperate to stop her.

Instead, he caught Tilda's attention. Her oily lips pressed tightly together, and she ripped the suitcase away from Sera's hands. Sera took a step back but Tilda clutched her arm, too, and started dragging her away.

As Riq continued running, the SQ men came through the columns, aiming directly for him. With them on one side and the lake in the other, Riq had a choice to make: run away and save himself, or run toward Tilda and risk being captured again.

They were trapped. But he knew what he had to do.

∞

"Sera, no!"

Recognizing Riq's voice, Sera looked over her shoulder and saw her friend racing toward her. Tilda actually hissed as she released Sera's arm and turned to run, still clutching the suitcase tightly. Riq obviously wanted to chase after her, but two burly men were running toward them, reeking of the SQ. So while Tilda bolted with the suitcase, Sera pulled Riq with her in the other direction.

"You escaped?" Sera asked Riq as they ran. She was beyond relieved about that.

"From those two guys chasing us," Riq said.

Sera glanced behind them, but the men weren't there. They had disappeared with Tilda. "I think they're gone."

Riq slowed, then stopped and looked carefully around them. When he was satisfied they were safe, he looked back at her with lips turned down and eyes that were clearly angry. Sera had expected gratitude from him. Not anger.

"You never should've come," he said.

"To save your life?" Sera said. "Yeah, so sorry about that."

"You saved my life, but at what price?" Riq drew in a breath. "You've given Tilda the power to destroy the world."

"She would've killed you if I didn't meet her."

"I'm a Hystorian, Sera. Protecting history from the SQ is more important than any of our lives. My life especially."

Sera blinked hard, but her eyes were clear when she stared back at him. "Dak and I can't do this alone. If we lose you, we won't be able to protect history from a stiff breeze."

She saw Riq soften at that, and his eyes darted away a moment before he said, "Thanks for the rescue, really. But just think about all the damage Tilda can do now. With the Ring, she could undo everything we've done. Or worse, go to other times and create entirely new Breaks."

At that, Sera smiled. "I've learned a few tricks since becoming a spy, you know. The Infinity Ring is safely hidden in locker forty-three at the train station."

Riq broke into a grin as well. "What was in that suitcase, then?"

"Rocks." Sera giggled. "Tilda's about to discover she made a deal for a couple of dumb, heavy rocks."

The leaves on the other side of the hedge where they were talking rustled in the wind, a reminder they were still out in the open. Tilda and her thugs were somewhere nearby. It was time to go.

Besides, they had a war to win.

The Trojan Deception

DAK HAD spent most of the past few days keeping his head down and, whenever possible, keeping out of sight. He did whatever kitchen work was asked of him and slept in a pantry hidden behind large buckets of sugar and flour. It wasn't pleasant, but neither was getting caught by the SQ. Of the two, he knew which was worse.

That all changed one afternoon when word came that an officer upstairs wanted a cup of tea. Everyone was busy preparing for supper, and finally the woman who had hired him pointed at Dak and said, "You, boy, take it up to him."

Dak wanted to tell her no, for the very good reason that somewhere outside the kitchens were two people under orders from Tilda to shorten his life span significantly. But he also knew he wasn't there to hide. It was his job to make sure that the German military's leaders accepted Major Martin's papers as real. This was an opportunity to get closer to them.

So he gathered everything for the tea onto a tray and asked, "Who is this for?"

Don't say it's for Hitler, he thought. If it was, Dak would be sorely tempted to throw the hot tea on him, Mincemeat Man or not.

But it wasn't. "Colonel Von Roenne," came the answer. "He's in his office upstairs."

Dak rolled his eyes and walked into the hallway. Von Roenne hadn't exposed him to Cleo and Anton before, which was a good sign. But Dak was still struggling to remember the significance of Von Roenne's name. He wished he'd thought to pick up a history book or two while in the twenty-first century.

Once upstairs, he passed several closed doors and wondered who was inside. He passed some open doors, too. In one of them, several Nazi officers were engaged in a loud argument.

"Martin is nothing but a Trojan horse!" one of the men shouted. "The British are playing tricks just as the Romans once did."

"Greeks!" Dak said before he thought better of it. The men stopped and stared at him, then Dak clamped his mouth shut and passed the open door.

Okay, yes, maybe he shouldn't have said anything, but if they were going to discuss the Trojan horse, they ought to get their facts straight. Over three thousand years ago BC, the Greeks wanted to invade the city of Troy, but after ten years of fighting still couldn't get inside their walls. So they built a huge wooden horse and left it outside the city walls, then went away. The Trojans pulled the horse inside their gates as a prize of war. What the city didn't know was that the Greeks had hidden soldiers inside the wooden horse, who waited until everyone was asleep at night, then snuck out and opened the gates. The rest of their army entered, and Troy fell soon after.

Whether the story actually happened was debatable, but personally, Dak believed it. And he thought the comparison to Mincemeat Man was pretty fair, too. The British had given Germany something they'd think was a prize of war—a dead body with secret information attached. But that information could be as destructive to the Germans as the Greek soldiers were to Troy. Mincemeat Man really was a modern-day Trojan horse.

"If the British wanted to trick us, there are easier ways," another man argued.

"Major Kuhlenthal tells us he will have Martin's papers any day now," a third man said. "Let's see what they say and then we'll decide."

"Kuhlenthal is too desperate to please the Führer," the first man said. "He will want to believe the papers are true because he needs them to be true. We need a more reasonable evaluation."

"Colonel Von Roenne will look over the information," the third man said. "There are few people Hitler trusts more."

Hearing the colonel's name reminded Dak that he had better deliver the tea before the water got cold. He left the men arguing and walked the rest of the way to Von Roenne's office.

He knocked on the door and heard a quick "Come in." Dak carefully balanced the heavy tray on one hand while he turned the doorknob and entered. But for all that, he nearly dropped it anyway once he looked up. Staring back at him, on either side of Von Roenne's desk, were Anton and Cleo.

Dak froze, unsure of what to do. It was too late to pretend he didn't know who they were. Should he drop the tray and run? Expose their SQ connections to Von Roenne? Maybe the colonel already knew. Maybe that's why he had called Dak here.

Anton and Cleo grinned wickedly when they recognized him, but Von Roenne didn't seem to notice. He motioned for Dak to bring the tray over to him, and then apologized for not having any to offer the others in the room.

"Shall I send this boy to bring more tea?" he asked politely.

"No," Anton said, staring down at Dak. "We can get whatever we want from him later on. And we will." His grin widened, but not in a pleasant way.

Von Roenne shifted the tray on his desk and several papers fell onto the floor near Dak. "Pick them up, will you, boy?" he asked.

Dak dropped to his knees to straighten the papers that had fallen. One, right on top, was printed with purple ink on a half sheet of thin, cream-colored paper. It was a telegram—sort of like text messaging for the 1940s. It read:

```
Col Von Roenne: Will have papers soon.
Will offer evaluation but hope you agree.
Maj Kuhlenthal
```

Dak figured this was probably the note that had started the argument back in that other room. He'd heard Kuhlenthal's name before, how powerful he eventually became in the war. This telegraph certainly had to be referring to Major Martin's papers.

Dak finished straightening the rest of the pile, then got to his feet and put it on the desk. Von Roenne noticed the telegram on top and looked up as if to ask whether Dak had read the telegram. But he didn't actually ask, and Dak wasn't about to volunteer the information. He only backed up and said, "May I go now?"

"You may," Von Roenne said.

"We'd better be leaving, too," Cleo said, keeping one eye on Dak.

"Not yet," Von Roenne said. "I have a few more questions first."

"Very well." She seemed irritated, but clearly had to do as Von Roenne ordered. Before Dak left, she turned to him and said, "I will want some tea when I'm finished here. I'll know where to find you when I'm ready."

Dak left the office, but he wasn't going back to the kitchens now. Maybe not ever. Every part of him wanted to leave the bunker at once and run for his life. But he was a spy now, and he had to finish his mission.

If this Major Kuhlenthal would have the papers soon, and if it was Von Roenne's job to decide whether they were real, then Dak had to get closer to Von Roenne. He found a small closet not far from Von Roenne's office and ducked inside, then closed the door after him. When Kuhlenthal sent the papers, the men in the office would begin arguing about them again. And that would be his sign that it was time to come out and convince one of Hitler's most trusted men to let his country lose a world war.

Kuhlenthal's Request

SERA AND Riq spent the rest of the afternoon near the German Embassy, where they discovered one interesting fact: Madrid loved gossip. The people here devoured it the way rabbits eat carrots. Everyone had his or her own tidbit of news to share in exchange for a friend's even juicier morsel. The two watched different pairs of people come and go from the embassy, heads inclined toward each other to share the latest scoop. And nobody seemed to care if they were talking near a young girl and boy engaged in a game of jacks. Sera and Riq might have looked like they were playing, but both had their ears tuned in to every word that was spoken near them.

"Nobody works harder than Kuhlenthal at spying on us," one Spanish officer said laughingly to another. "Does he think we don't know who he is? He's lucky so many of us support the Nazis, or he wouldn't get very far."

"I've heard he has Jewish blood, from a grand-mother," the officer's companion said. "Can you believe it, a Jewish-born Nazi? Imagine if Hitler knew about that."

Minutes later, two men in Nazi uniforms passed them. "Personally, I doubt the papers are real," one of them said. "But that's for Kuhlenthal to decide, not us."

"He had better hope he gets this right," responded the other. "He's fallen for Allied tricks before. And yet, if the papers are real and Kuhlenthal backs them, he will become the Führer's favorite spy."

Sera looked over at Riq and frowned. This spy business was starting to mess with her head.

Britain needed everyone to think they were desperate to get Martin's papers back.

But they couldn't actually succeed in getting them back. At least, not until Germany saw them.

The papers had to look as if they were written in a code, to protect them in case they were found.

Yet the code had to be easy for Germany to figure out, although not so easy that it would look as if Britain was trying to trick them.

And if she and Riq were going to be helpful, they had to persuade Kuhlenthal to trust them. If they pushed too hard, though, he might suspect something. So how were they supposed to convince him?

After several hours, Riq and Sera had nearly given up hope of even seeing Kuhlenthal that day. Maybe he'd come tomorrow. Or maybe never. Sera was standing up to leave when she heard footsteps behind her and turned.

Kuhlenthal was right behind her, but his blue eyes were focused on Riq. "Who is this?"

"We both speak English," Sera said. "But my friend here can speak a dozen other languages perfectly."

"Two dozen," Riq corrected, then shrugged when Sera glanced back at him. "I've been practicing in my spare time."

Kuhlenthal frowned. "We have other Nazis who can read English, of course, but if I let them see the letters, they'll tell Hitler that *they* solved this mystery, not me. You understand that I can't allow anyone else to read them until I've made my report."

Sera nodded. Her heart was racing, though she wasn't sure if it was from excitement or fear. Maybe it was both.

"You can trust us," Riq said. "Besides, even if we tried to report back to Hitler, he'd never believe a couple of kids."

Kuhlenthal seemed to like that. He stepped closer to them and said, "The wet ink ran in a few places and I can't make out the words. I must get a report back to Germany immediately. Can you help me read it?"

Sera and Riq followed Kuhlenthal into the German Embassy. He led them downstairs into a narrow, poorly lit hallway, and on their way, explained that the Spanish officials had cleverly managed to remove the letters from the envelopes without breaking the seals. The letters had been dried and then given to him — but only for a single hour. There had been just enough time to photograph the letters before returning them, and now the photos had been developed.

"What will happen to the letters now?" Sera asked.

"Spain will soak them in seawater again, then refold them and replace them in the envelopes. They will lock the briefcase and return it to Britain as if none of this had ever happened." He chuckled. "Sometimes I have thought the Allies are very clever. But they underestimated the reach of the Nazis. They will continue forward with their battle plans without any idea that we know their secrets."

Sera cast an eye at Riq, who only lifted his eyebrows in response. It was a most dangerous game of cat and mouse. Both Germany and Britain believed they were tricking the other side. And in the next great battle between the two, one would be proven right, and the other would suffer a major defeat that could cost thousands of lives.

Kuhlenthal put his hand on a doorknob, but before opening it turned to Sera and Riq. "The only person who will ever know you saw these is me," he said. "So if you try any tricks, nothing can save you."

Sera swallowed hard and nodded, then Kuhlenthal led them into a small room with portable lights set up to brighten it. The papers that must have been there only a short time ago were now replaced with enlarged black-and-white photographs. The photographer had been thorough. Every word of the letters was in at least one of his pictures.

Kuhlenthal motioned them in closer, then spread out the photos so they could be better examined.

The first photo was Martin's military identification card. The person pictured on the identification looked very similar to the body that Sera had seen during the postmortem, but it couldn't be the same person. She knew the British had gotten Martin's body after he was already dead, while this man was very much alive. Sera had once heard that everyone in the world had someone out there who looked exactly like them — a doppel-ganger — and if that was true, the British had somehow managed to find that person for their Mincemeat Man.

Kuhlenthal lifted the identity card to Sera. "You've seen his body for yourself," he said. "Is this the same man?"

Sera pretended to study the picture, but of course she already knew how she'd answer. "The body had decomposed from its time in the water," she said. "But this picture looks just like him." She figured that was truthful enough.

Another set of photos documented a letter to Major Martin from his father, scolding him for not being as responsible as he should. Then there was a loving letter from a woman who was engaged to marry Martin. That one looked as if it had been folded and unfolded many times—Sera liked that detail. Of course a man at war would reread that letter as often as possible.

Of more interest to the Germans, there was a note from Martin's commander warning the recipient that the papers he was carrying were very important and secretive. It also made a request for Martin to return with some sardines, since they were hard to find in Britain. That was a bogus request, since whoever actually wrote the letter would have known Major Martin would not come back alive. He didn't even leave while still alive.

Along with that note was the heart of the entire Mincemeat Man plan: a letter from one British general to another. Sera read it as quickly as she could. It said that they hoped the Germans would believe Sicily was about to be attacked, but that the real invasion was for Greece. The letter had everything the Germans would need: the dates for the attack, the size of the invasion force, and the code names that would be used.

The risk was plain enough. If Germany didn't believe the Allies were going to invade Greece, then they would know quite a bit about the real invasion of Sicily.

Kuhlenthal pointed out a few words where the ink had run, and Riq and Sera were both quick to give their most honest opinions as to what was written there. When they were finished, Kuhlenthal pulled up a chair and leaned back, deep in thought, with his eyes closed and the fingertips of each hand pressed against one another. Riq and Sera waited in the awkward silence, unsure of what to do.

Finally, Kuhlenthal opened his eyes. "Why would the Allies want Greece?" he asked. "Sicily is far more important."

"But Sicily is too well defended," Riq said. "If the Allies take Greece, then they will be in a better position to attack Sicily later on."

"True." Kuhlenthal went back into deep thought, and after a moment he said, "A commander of the British army is having a hard time finding a simple can of sardines? Are things so bad in Britain that even a general can't have his treat?"

"Sardines are the least of Britain's problems," Sera said. "Besides, they smell bad anyway."

"What smells?" Kuhlenthal asked. "The sardines or the British?"

Riq and Sera laughed, but not really. The situation was far too dangerous and the joke just wasn't that funny.

Kuhlenthal quickly grew serious again. "I wouldn't dare to share this secret with anyone else — most of the Nazis here would be very glad to see me fail and take my place — but I need these papers to be real. It has been a long time since I have sent anything useful to Hitler. He is becoming . . . impatient with me."

That was their chance, Sera realized. Kuhlenthal would believe the letters simply because he wanted so badly for them to be real. For the sake of his career, and maybe his life, he *needed* them to be real.

Which led her to a worse idea. For a long time, Sera had believed that if they fixed history and made everything okay, that her family would be there when she came home, happy and healthy and alive. Even with Tilda's recent accusations, Sera realized she *still* expected a happy reunion at the end of all this. But maybe her visions of a happy ending weren't any more real than Major Martin's papers. Maybe she only believed it would come true because she wanted so desperately for it to come true.

Suddenly, Kuhlenthal clapped his hands together and stood up, then began gathering the photos. "I must catch a flight back to Germany at once," he said. "I will deliver these to the Führer myself."

"What are you going to tell him?" Riq asked.

"My report will be as balanced as I can make it," Kuhlenthal answered. "But if I am to convince the Führer that the Allies are invading Greece, I will need to get his most trusted man on my side: Colonel Von Roenne."

18

Sera's Suspicions

THEY HAD done as much as they possibly could, and with that, Sera was more than happy to get herself and Riq out of there. Kuhlenthal spooked her. He wasn't SQ, but that didn't make him any less dangerous. As far as she was concerned, she and Riq had done everything they could to convince him to believe Mincemeat Man. The rest was up to Dak.

"I wish to pay you for your services," Kuhlenthal said. "Whatever Clauss gave you, I will give you the same."

Sera started to tell him no thanks, but Riq quickly accepted, then looked at Sera as if to remind her that Kuhlenthal would trust them more if he could pay them. Besides, they needed some money if they were going to eat in the next few days.

Eating was a fine idea, but so was being alive, and Sera wasn't entirely sure that was Kuhlenthal's plan.

Kuhlenthal escorted Riq and Sera outside, leading them away from the building and down a steep hill where it was dark and they were alone. Sera didn't like the feel of this, not at all, but how could she warn Riq of her concerns without alerting Kuhlenthal?

"I know there are many spies like me." Kuhlenthal's dark expression was lit by the bright moon overhead. "And then there are double agents, who pretend to be on my side, but work for the enemy."

"We helped you," Sera said.

"And I told you, I don't need the help of a young girl." He turned and pulled some money from his pocket, then held it out to them. "This will pay for your silence, I think."

Sera stood in place, still suspicious, but Riq thanked the major and stepped forward to accept the money. When he reached out his hand, Sera caught a glint of metal in the moonlight. She cried, "Riq, he has a knife!"

Riq swerved around, but Kuhlenthal grabbed his arm and yanked Riq toward him. Sera noticed a fallen tree branch near her feet. She picked it up and swung it at Kuhlenthal like she was batting for a home run.

She connected with a satisfying crack, and the branch broke in two.

Riq fell forward onto the ground, clutching at his side, and Kuhlenthal rolled backward down the steep hill. Down where Sera figured she and Riq were supposed to have rolled instead, probably not to have been found for days.

"C'mon," Sera yelled, starting to run up the hill.

But Riq, still on his knees, was gathering up the money that had scattered when Kuhlenthal had fallen. "We'll need this!"

He was right about that, and Sera hurried back to help him grab what they could before Kuhlenthal made it up the hillside again. They heard his growls somewhere below them, and set off as quickly as they could run.

Neither of them stopped until they were far away from Kuhlenthal, the Ministry building, and anyone who even looked like a spy.

Only then did Riq sink against a shop wall, still holding his side. "He cut me."

"What?" Sera went to her knees beside him. His shirt had a small slice in it, but only a thin trickle of blood was showing.

"How bad is it?" Riq asked.

"Pretty awful," Sera said, hiding her smile. "You'll need surgery, but since we can't trust the doctors here, I'll have to do it myself. Do you happen to have a needle and thread?"

"Oh, no you don't!" Riq practically leapt to his feet and twisted around to inspect the damage for himself. Then he looked up. "Yeah, that was funny. Now I can see why you and Dak get along."

"Sorry," Sera said, laughing now. "Does it hurt?"

"Yeah," Riq said. "But I guess it's not as bad as I thought. Let's get out of here."

"But to where?" Sera asked. "It's after curfew, so we shouldn't be out."

She followed after Riq as he started walking. "We passed a quiet alley a little ways back," he said. "It's a warm night and the alley should give us some protection in case Kuhlenthal goes poking around. We'll take shifts staying awake tonight and figure out what to do next after we've had some sleep."

They didn't get much sleep, but the following morning, Sera and Riq each bought a warm, sugary churro and talked over what they should do next.

"We've done as much as we can," Riq said. "Kuhlenthal will take the papers to Germany and the rest will be up to Dak."

"*If* Dak even stuck around," Sera said worriedly. Riq had told her about Tilda's orders to have the SQ in Berlin find him, which had put a knot in her stomach that wouldn't go away. "I think we need to go to Germany," she added. "We have to see this through, and besides, we have to find Dak."

Riq nodded, but Sera saw the doubt in his eyes. "Kuhlenthal mentioned that he had to get a flight into Germany. It's probably on a military plane, so we can't follow that way."

"I know," Sera said. "But we have to get the Infinity Ring from the train station anyway. We'll use the money from Kuhlenthal to catch the next train out of here, so we probably won't be too far behind him."

"If Dak is still okay, our going to Germany might make things worse for him," Riq warned.

"I know." Sera drew in a breath. "If he's undercover, we could expose him. But we're not warping out of here without Dak. We have to take the risk."

They took a taxi to the train station, always with one eye on the cars around them to be sure they weren't followed. Once they arrived, Sera led Riq to some lockers.

"I knew I couldn't bring the Infinity Ring anywhere near that park," she explained. "It was too dangerous to just hide it under a bush or something, and if I had it on me, Tilda would've known it wasn't in that suitcase."

"But these lockers don't look all that secure," Riq said. "Anyone with a basic knowledge of lock picking could get inside one."

"Maybe," Sera said. "But nobody other than us knows the Infinity Ring's bag is here, so they'd have no reason to break in."

She inserted a key into the lock and opened the door. The Infinity Ring's bag was there, exactly as she had left it.

But everything wasn't *exactly* as it had been. Just as a spy would, Sera had plucked a hair from her head and laid it over the top of the satchel. If someone wanted to open the satchel, they'd have to move the hair to do so. And to Sera's dismay, she noticed now that the strand of hair was *under* the satchel. Had someone else been inside this locker?

Sera lunged for the bag and pulled it open, revealing the Infinity Ring — safe and sound.

"What's wrong?" Riq asked.

"Nothing," Sera said quickly. But she wondered: What if Tilda had somehow known the Infinity Ring was in here? Was it possible she had broken in and used it?

Sera sighed. She hated to admit it, but it was possible. However, it was also unlikely. If Tilda or anyone else had gone to so much trouble to steal the Ring, why bother returning it? Maybe someone had broken into the locker for valuables, and assumed the Ring was a worthless toy.

"C'mon," Sera said, lifting the satchel and returning it to her belt, "we've got a train to catch."

Minutes later as their train rolled out of the station, Riq leaned over to Sera and said, "It won't be as easy as you think to waltz into Germany. Are you sure it's worth all this trouble to get Dak?"

Sera smiled at his joke, but the knot in her stomach returned again. If Dak was . . . If the SQ had already gotten to Dak, then everything they had done so far would have been a waste of time.

Dak and the Wolf

DAK WASN'T sure how long he stayed hidden in that closet. He knew when Anton and Cleo left Von Roenne's office because they walked past, and Anton muttered something about "Gotta find that kid today." And Cleo then said something about waiting for him to show up near the kitchen.

Words like that made it a lot easier to stay right where he was. And except for the fact that he was getting tired of standing, it wasn't the worst place. In the darkness, he started counting backward from 1943, listing off major world events from each year, like any ordinary history genius might do for fun. He got briefly stuck on 1938, until he remembered a radio show called "War of the Worlds" that had been performed to sound like a news alert about an alien invasion. Even though there were several announcements during the broadcast about it only being a performance, it set the entire country into a panic for hours. People packed up and left their homes, fired guns into the air to warn away the aliens, and prepared themselves for the end of the world.

Dak frowned at that. There was certainly no alien attack, but the end of the world was coming if he didn't gather up some courage and leave this closet.

He slowly opened the closet door and looked both ways before sneaking out. It was late and most people had gone home. But in Von Roenne's office, Dak could hear the clatter of a typewriter.

He balled up his fists, took a deep breath, and then knocked on Von Roenne's door.

"Come in." As usual, Von Roenne's voice was terse, but not unkind.

When Dak entered, Von Roenne looked up, arched an eyebrow when he recognized Dak, then swiveled his chair away from his typewriter and clasped his hands.

"You again?" Von Roenne seemed curious, although Dak wasn't sure if that was a good thing or not. "What do you want?"

"A few days ago, you said I owe you a favor. I want to repay you now. I can help here in your office, with any jobs you need."

Von Roenne stared at him a moment, then pushed his glasses higher on his nose. "Please have a seat. What is your name?"

"Dak."

"An unusual name. Are you German?"

"There's German blood on my mother's side." However, Dak failed to mention that his great-grandfather was born near London, and in fact, was serving in the British navy at this time. He figured Von Roenne didn't need that much of his family background.

"I'm told a housekeeper brought you here to help in the kitchen."

"Yes, sir."

Von Roenne leaned in closer. "But I suspect there's more to you than that. We both know about the man and woman in these headquarters who seem to have nothing better to do than look for you. I suspect if you're caught, our housekeeper will need another kitchen boy. Why is that? Did you steal something from them?"

"No, sir."

"Did you cause them any trouble?"

"No, sir." It was actually just the opposite.

Von Roenne frowned at him. "Then are you here as a spy?"

Despite trying to hide any reaction, Dak was taken aback by the question and his eyes widened. He tried to speak, but his mouth felt like it was full of cotton, and his tongue felt roughly the size of Everest.

Von Roenne leaned back. "Ah, so the Allies are using children now to spy on us. Is that because they have so much trust in you, or so little fear of us?"

"The Allies have no idea I'm here. They don't know anything about me."

"Then why are you here?" Impatient for an answer, Von Roenne said, "You'll talk to me, or I'll turn you over to that pair who are probably searching this building for you right now."

"I – I'm not . . . I just –" Which was as far as Dak got before the cotton mouth started up again.

Obviously, he couldn't tell one of Hitler's most trusted advisers that he was here from the future. The idea of what Hitler could do if he got control of time travel was terrifying.

Nor could he tell Von Roenne about Mincemeat Man. The last thing he needed was for the collapse of the Allies in World War II to be blamed on him. He would be in the history books one day – Dak was sure of that – but not for being the one to destroy the free world. No way.

But he was having trouble coming up with any reason why he might be here otherwise. The obvious thought was to convince Von Roenne that he wanted to join up with the Nazis, that he believed in their cause and wanted to help, even if he was too young to be a soldier.

But there was no way Dak would tell a lie like that. Even to save the mission or to save his own life, Dak would never let those words come out of his mouth. Von Roenne seemed like a decent enough person. But he was fighting for the wrong side, and taking orders from truly evil men.

The Führer, Adolf Hitler, was responsible for millions of deaths on the battlefield, both from those fighting for him and against him. Beyond that, before the war ended, he would be responsible for the deaths of over six million Jewish people. Innocent families who would be rounded up, held in concentration camps, and eventually killed for no crime other than who they were by faith and by heritage.

Thinking of them, Dak was surer than ever that Mincemeat Man had to succeed. It wouldn't save all those lives, but at least the Allies would win in the end, and those lost lives could forever serve as a reminder of how evil must never be allowed to spread.

"All right, if you won't talk, then you'll come with me." Von Roenne stood and walked from behind his desk over to Dak.

"You can't give me to Anton and Cleo," Dak said. "They'll kill me if you do."

Von Roenne placed his hands on his hips. "Then why—"

He was interrupted by another knock on his door. Dak looked all around for any way he might escape if it was Anton and Cleo returning. He could dive out Von Roenne's window, which always looked pretty cool in action movies. But in real life, he'd never do that. The glass would get him all cut up, and he'd probably break a leg landing on the cement below. If it were them, his only choice would be to run and hope like crazy to be fast enough that they couldn't grab him.

Dak pressed his toes against the ground, ready to push off and run.

Von Roenne invited whoever had knocked to enter, but rather than the two Time Wardens, it was a group of Nazi soldiers who entered instead. *Oh, good,* Dak thought. *More Nazis.*

"The Führer to see Colonel Von Roenne," one of the soldiers announced.

Dak forgot anything he had ever known about running and instead backed up behind Von Roenne. Now entering the room was none other than Adolf Hitler.

Von Roenne's Rescue

COLONEL VON Roenne stood at attention and raised his right arm straight in front of him. *"Heil, mein* Führer!" He nudged at Dak to do the same, but Dak could not, *would not,* do it.

Everything Dak had ever read about Adolf Hitler flooded his mind. How he'd wanted to be an artist when he was young, but failed. How he fought for Germany in the First World War and felt betrayed when his leaders surrendered. The months he spent in prison for trying to overthrow the government, and then afterward, how he built up his Nazi party to take over the government in a legal way. Once he had control, he took over Austria without firing a single shot. But when he invaded Poland, the Second World War began.

Hitler was of average height and build, but people may not have noticed since their attention likely went straight to his face. His thin brown hair was parted at the side and combed neatly across his forehead, and he had a small square mustache above his lip. His eyes were cold and stern, and seemed to bore through anything he stared at.

Luckily, Hitler gave Dak all the notice that he'd give a chair in the room. His eyes flicked over Dak and settled on Von Roenne.

"Have the papers arrived yet?" Hitler asked.

"No, *mein* Führer. But I'm waiting here in case Major Kuhlenthal arrives late tonight. We only know that the papers indicate the Allies will attack Greece and not Sicily."

"It sounds too easy," Hitler said. "That a dead British officer should wash up on the shores of Spain with the most top secret of plans?"

"I also have my suspicions," Von Roenne said. "But until we have those papers, we cannot know exactly what the plans are, or if they are real."

"I'm told that Captain Clauss got very close to the body, and that it is certain to have drowned off the coast of Spain."

"He was there for the examination?" Von Roenne asked.

"No, but he had an informant who was there, a Spanish girl who assisted the doctor. Afterward, she told him everything she had seen."

Dak smiled to himself. Sera had a primarily Mayan heritage, not Spanish, but it must have been her at the autopsy. Sometimes she was so cool!

Von Roenne sighed. "Then it sounds hopeful. But even if the papers are an Allied trick, this is still very good news for us. If they are real, then our army must move to Greece. The Allies will be surprised to see us there. It will be an easy win for Germany."

Hitler cocked an eyebrow. "And if the plans are fake?"

"Then I will know." Von Roenne spoke so confidently that Dak became worried. He added, "If the plans are fake, then it will be obvious that the Allies are going to Sicily. Our forces are so strong there, the Allies won't have a chance. Either way, the coming battle will seal Germany as an eventual winner in this war."

Hitler nodded without smiling, and it occurred to Dak that he had rarely seen any photo of the man smiling. He *could* smile, Dak assumed. The muscles worked the same as for anyone else, but he chose not to. He wanted to be seen as fierce, bold, and someone to fear. A wolf.

Hitler began to leave, then finally noticed Dak in the room. "Is this a houseboy for you?" he asked Von Roenne.

"I am considering whether to allow him to work for me," Von Roenne answered. "At least, until he is old enough to train as a soldier."

"He's already old enough," Hitler said. "We might not send him to war yet, but he can train now. From the Nazis, he must learn the true history of our people."

Dak felt his muscles tightening and tried not to look angry. This man had nothing to teach him about history.

Hitler stepped closer and looked him over. "Your mother and father would be proud of you, boy, to hear that you have joined our great cause."

"My parents have been missing for some time, sir," Dak said. "I am alone." The words echoed in his ears. He was the most alone he had ever been in his entire life. And not particularly comforted by the company he was currently keeping.

Hitler addressed Von Roenne. "When we own the youth, we own the future. Have this boy sent to begin his training tomorrow. I'll personally find a place for him within the ranks of the Hitler Youth."

"I won't go." Maybe it was stupid to speak, but on this issue, Dak refused to be silent.

Hitler opened his mouth to say something, probably to drag Dak kicking and screaming into those camps if necessary, but Von Roenne spoke first. "Pardon him, *mein* Führer, the boy only meant he cannot go. He owes me some work, and I know you expect our boys to pay their debts. Besides, he'll get no better preparation to become a Nazi than with me."

"Very well," Hitler said, ignoring Dak again. "I expect your evaluation of Kuhlenthal's papers by tomorrow."

"It will be done," Von Roenne said.

It took a full minute after Hitler left before Dak felt he could breathe normally again. Von Roenne had returned to his desk with Dak fixed in his gaze.

"Thank you," Dak said.

Von Roenne didn't flinch. He only continued to stare. It made Dak uncomfortable, and he shifted his weight.

Finally, Von Roenne spoke. "You may wonder why I kept you here."

"Yes, sir."

"It's because I cannot quite figure you out, and I'm curious. I believe you are telling me the truth about yourself, but not the whole truth."

Dak stayed silent. If he had wanted to argue the point, he might have said he felt exactly the same way about Von Roenne.

"And if I were going to have a houseboy, I'd have preferred one who could safely leave this room to fetch me some tea."

"There are other things I can do for you," Dak said.

"Such as?"

Dak shuffled his feet on the floor a moment before speaking. Finally, he said, "I'm a Hystorian. I know a lot about the past . . . and the future." It was a risk to say that, and he knew Riq would be punching him right now to hear Dak identify himself so openly to a high-level Nazi. But he had to know if Von Roenne was on his side.

Von Roenne only arched an eyebrow and said, "A historian? Well, boy, you may know the past, but the future has yet to be written."

Dak felt deflated to hear that. At least Von Roenne wasn't SQ, or he'd have known what Dak was talking about, but he wasn't a Hystorian either.

"All right," Von Roenne added. "If you're a historian, then perhaps you can be helpful when Major Kuhlenthal arrives tonight. In the meantime, you can make yourself useful and clean up my office. If the Führer returns and sees you resting, he will take you with him whether I like it or not. And I promise that once he gets hold of your mind, he will never let it go."

"Does he have your mind, sir?" Dak asked.

Von Roenne only looked back at him with a frown, and then returned to his work at his desk.

And that was really the big question, Dak figured. Because if Von Roenne was as loyal to Hitler as he claimed to be, then Dak didn't stand a chance.

Out of the Frying Pan

DUSK WAS setting in once Riq awoke to the announcement that the train's conductor would be coming through the cabin soon to check passports. He hadn't asked for them at France, and so Riq had forgotten about the chance they might be needed. But if they were caught on board without passports, they risked being arrested in Berlin. An image of the concentration camps passed through his mind. The horrors that happened there were hard enough to have read about in school. He didn't want to see them. And he couldn't let the Nazis get the Infinity Ring.

Sera had also been awoken by the announcement and was barely halfway through a yawn when Riq grabbed her hand. "C'mon."

Sera followed him out of her seat. "Where are we going?"

"You heard the conductor. He's coming to look at passports."

"Now? Are we in Berlin?"

"No, but by the time the conductor checks all the passengers, we will be."

The passenger cars were connected to one another by covered vestibules that made it safe to move from one car to another. As the conductor entered their car from the front, Riq pressed Sera toward the vestibule behind them.

"We can't avoid him forever," Sera mumbled. "And we're almost at the back of the train anyway."

"Don't worry," Riq said. "I have an idea."

Once they were in the vestibule, Riq shut the connecting doors. The vestibule was constructed of thick steel, but an access door was provided to allow engineers in and out in case of emergencies. As far as Riq was concerned, this was a pretty serious emergency. The clatter of the train upon the tracks was louder here, which didn't make it any easier to do what had to be done next. He pulled the door's lever, hoping it wouldn't alert the engineer as would happen on a modern train, and then slid the door open.

Sera stared down at the ground, moving so fast the rocks and brush were just a blur beneath them. "You're crazy if you think I'm gonna jump."

"We're not jumping," Riq said. "But when we boarded, I noticed a ladder on the back of this train. You just have to swing your body around to reach it. I'll hold on to you and keep you safe. Then you help me get onto the ladder. We'll ride the rest of the way from there."

Sera smirked. "Jump onto a ladder while we're moving at a hundred miles an hour? What happens to our kinetic energy if we fall?"

"Forget physics and ask yourself what happens when that conductor asks for our passports."

"Better to be arrested than do a high-speed hello to the ground!"

Voices from inside the car in front of them grew loud enough to be heard even from where Riq stood. He and Sera peered through a small window and saw two young men standing in the aisle. "No passports!" The conductor blew on a whistle and immediately two Nazi soldiers entered. They each grabbed one of the young men and roughly escorted them into a forward car. Riq didn't even want to think about what would happen to them next.

"That'll be us if we don't get on that ladder," Riq whispered.

He and Sera darted back from the window as the conductor looked their way. Riq doubted he could have seen them — it was dark in the vestibule, so they should've been lost in the shadows. But then the conductor straightened his jacket and started walking toward them.

"Now!" Riq said.

He put his hands on Sera's waist and planted his feet to keep himself inside the vestibule while she leaned out from the train.

"I can see the ladder," Sera said. "But I can't quite reach it."

So Riq held Sera with one hand and with the other, he braced himself to lean even farther out of the vestibule. The train lurched over a bump in the tracks, and Sera was jolted out of his grasp.

"Sera!" he cried.

After a terrifying moment, she peeked back at him. "I almost fell just now. And just so you know, this is worse than all of Dak's bad ideas put together! Now give me your hand."

Riq squeezed out of the train as far as he dared and slid the door most of the way closed behind him. With his longer arms, he reached over to the ladder without too much trouble and felt Sera's hands on his, supporting his weight as he swung toward her. Riq's feet slipped and slid on the ladder rung, but Sera immediately moved her hand to his belt and pulled him up until he was stable.

Riq tried to reach back to shut the door, but just as he did the conductor entered the vestibule. Riq motioned for Sera to climb, so they would be out of sight if the conductor somehow peered around the corner. They heard him grunt and pull the emergency door open wider. A long moment of silence followed while he was probably looking around for any sign of why it might be open. Finally, he closed the door and Riq was sure he heard it latch again.

Riq and Sera were near the top of the ladder now. Wind, dust, and occasional bits of gravel rushed at them, making it impossible to keep their eyes open, and it wasn't much easier to breathe.

"We'll be safe here," Riq said.

"If we don't freeze or fall off or get whacked by something flying through the air first," Sera said. "Anyone who knows Newton's third law of motion knows how dangerous this is."

"Uh, anyone who knows anything would know how dangerous this is," Riq countered.

Sera adjusted her grip again. "I knew getting into Berlin would be hard, but I didn't picture it like this."

"That's funny," Riq said, "because when I pictured it, I thought things would be even worse."

As the ride continued, Riq gradually changed his mind. It was better out here than under arrest by the Nazis, but not easier. His shoulder, which had finally stopped bothering him from when he dislocated it in Baghdad, was starting to ache again. His eyes were dry and dusty, and he had so much grit in his mouth he could taste it. But Sera was holding on tight with her elbows locked on the ladder and face nestled into her shoulder. She didn't complain or whine, even though he knew her arms must be getting as tired as his were. If she didn't complain, he knew he couldn't either. At least, not out loud.

At last, the train began to slow as it pulled into a

station just outside Berlin. Riq and Sera jumped from the ladder before it had completely stopped so they would be out of sight from the people standing on the platform. Looking back over his shoulder as they walked off, Riq decided that was a good idea anyway. He saw a lot of Nazi uniforms on the platform and was in no hurry to get any closer to them.

Then one of the Nazis looked directly at them and whispered to the others with him. They turned to look at Riq and Sera and one of them reached for the baton at his waist.

"We've got trouble." Riq grabbed Sera's arm and started to lead her away. "Just act casual."

"Casual?" Sera hissed. "Nazi soldiers are watching us and you want me to act casual?"

Pretending to wave to someone on the train, Riq turned momentarily and saw the soldiers picking up speed behind them. Casual wasn't going to work. This was quickly turning into a full-scale reason to panic.

"Get ready to run on three," he muttered to Sera. "One. Two. Now!"

Sera was already on her way when he took off. But where were they supposed to go?

"Over here!" A woman stood in front of a small alcove. She was Sera's height and wore a tight bun, and she carried with her a black umbrella that she opened and held behind her. "Get behind me!"

Riq looked at Sera, who shrugged and got behind the wide umbrella. He wasn't sure it was safe, but he knew for a fact that getting caught by the Nazis was worse. So he followed and stood with Sera, both of them pressed tightly against the wall.

"*Guten Abend,*" an officer said to the woman. Riq's translator had kicked in by then, but he already knew that was the phrase for "good evening." The officer continued, "Have you seen two children run past here, a boy and girl? They snuck rides on the train."

"I did see them!" The woman pointed down the platform. "They ran that way only a minute ago. If you hurry, you'll catch them!"

When the officers had run past, the woman lowered her umbrella and turned to them. "Stole a ride aboard a train?"

"No!" Sera said. "We had tickets. We just . . . we just had a problem along the way."

The woman pressed her thin lips together until they nearly disappeared, and then said, "The Nazis should have more important work than chasing children around. Be more careful next time, my dears."

She started to walk away, but Riq said, "Maybe you can help us again." He pulled out a paper from his pocket with an address written on it for the Abwehr Headquarters in Berlin. As the headquarters for German spies, this was where Kuhlenthal would take Major Martin's papers. It was also where Dak had planned to go. Riq held the paper out to the woman. "Can you tell us how to get here?"

She looked at the address. "Abwehr? That's no place for children. Especially at night."

Sera's hand went to the sack holding the Infinity Ring. "We're only meeting a friend near there. Nothing special."

Now the woman smiled down at them. "It's nearly curfew, and you shouldn't be out on the streets. You'll never make it there on time."

Riq eyed Sera. "Maybe we could sleep here at the train station tonight."

Sera's expression begged Riq to find another way. He knew she was worried about Dak, and she was right. They couldn't stay here.

The woman puckered her lips while she thought, then said, "My husband is waiting outside with our car. I suppose we could drive you to the headquarters, if you are sure your friend will be there to meet you."

"We'll be able to find him," Riq said, as much for Sera's benefit as the woman's.

The woman escorted Riq and Sera out of the train station and led them to a car waiting near the curb. After she talked to her husband through the window, she nodded at them and opened the door to the backseat, ushering them forward.

Riq began to climb in, then froze. Behind him, Sera did the exact same thing.

Already seated inside, another woman lowered a mirror as she finished applying oil-black lipstick around her mouth. She eyed the kids with a cold glare that turned Riq's feet to ice.

"Get in," she said. "We've been waiting for you."

Into the Fire

SERA'S INSTINCT was to run, and she knew Riq would be right on her heels. But before she could move, the driver stepped from the car to stand directly behind her, casting an imposing shadow. It was Anton, and he pushed both her and Riq forward, forcing them into the car. She considered yelling for help, but who was going to come? Those Nazis? They weren't any better.

Riq went in first and Sera sat against the outside door. Quietly, she slipped the Infinity Ring's bag between her seat and the door. If they had a chance during the ride, she would pass it to Riq to slip inside his jacket, where it would be less noticeable.

"Where are you taking us?" Riq asked.

"Abwehr Headquarters," Tilda said. "Isn't that where you wanted to go? Isn't that where we'll find your friend Dak?"

"We've already found him!" the woman with the

bun said from the front seat. "The minute he steps out of Colonel Von Roenne's office, he's ours."

"But he isn't stepping out of there," Tilda said. "You had plenty of chances before! That boy is smarter than you gave him credit for, Cleo."

"It's not that," Anton said. "We can't just go wherever we want in the building. Even the SQ doesn't have that kind of freedom with the Nazis."

"But an eleven-year-old boy does?" Tilda asked. "Well, it doesn't matter now, because once Dak knows I have his two best friends, he'll do anything to save them." Her eyes flicked to Sera and Riq. "He'll even undo all the damage I'm sure you three kids have caused here."

"We're only fixing history back to how it's supposed to be!" Sera said. "It's the SQ that interfered."

"Anton and I have been spying on the British for years," the woman said. "And we've been spying on the Nazis since their rise to power. All of this was so that when the time came for us to turn the war to the advantage of the SQ, we would be ready. Nobody will win this conflict but us!"

"You're destroying the world!" Riq yelled. "Every time you pull history off course from how things are supposed to be, you destroy it a little more."

"I can save it," Tilda said. "I have the tools now . . . with me as the head of the SQ, not only in our present time, but in the past and for all of the future."

"There is no future," Sera said. "Not unless you let us go."

Tilda was joined in her laughter by the man and woman in the front seat. "Let you go?" Tilda asked. "After so much trouble to find you, why would I do that? I've been waiting for years to find you."

"Years?" Sera asked. That didn't make sense.

"In your travels, you went to the year 1850, in America," Tilda said. "Do you remember?"

Of course Sera remembered. In their work to save Harriet Tubman and the Underground Railroad, they had also played a role in saving one of Riq's relatives. When Riq saved Kissy and John from the SQ, he had done more than change their history. He had changed his own.

Sera turned to stare at Riq as all the pieces of his secret fell into place in her mind. Suddenly, she understood why he had refused to return to the present to get a new SQuare. Why he acted so gloomy every time they talked of their future lives. And why his Remnants were like black holes.

To save history, Riq might already have sacrificed himself.

He looked back at her, and without a word seemed to know why the tears had welled in her eyes. He only smiled grimly and gave her hand a squeeze.

"So what if we were in 1850?" Riq asked. "We've been a lot of places."

"Yes, but you met someone there," Tilda said. "Someone very important to me."

"Ilsa," Sera whispered.

Speaking the name sent a shudder down her spine. Ilsa had nearly destroyed the entire Underground Railroad. But even worse, she had gotten hold of the Infinity Ring long enough to travel forward in time with Sera to see the Cataclysm. Rarely a night passed when Sera didn't have a nightmare connected with what she had seen.

"Ilsa is my great-great-great-grandmother," Tilda explained. "Not the first in our family to be SQ, but certainly a fine role model to me."

"And are your other role models vultures and snakes?" Riq asked. "Because you seem to have a lot in common with them, too."

Tilda ignored him and continued. "After Ilsa had her experience of time travel with you, she wrote a letter about everything she knew, everything she had seen. It was passed to her daughter, and to hers, and so on, and eventually came to me. I never understood what it all meant, until after you disappeared from Hystorian headquarters. I was ready for you the next time you returned."

"If Ilsa wrote that letter, then she must have explained what the future is like," Sera said.

"Of course she did," Tilda said. "And now I know how to prevent it. I must destroy Aristotle, the interfering fool who started the Hystorians in the first place. If the Hystorians are not there to oppose the SQ at every turn, we can set history on its proper course much earlier and avoid all these Breaks you people like to go on about."

"That's not how it works," Sera said. "You've got it all backward."

Tilda only laughed. "Believe what you will, Sera. But the best thing you can do is give up now. Let Dak trade away this war to get you and Riq back, and then you three find a cozy place in time to enjoy the rest of your lives. It's better that way."

"I can't do that," Sera said fiercely. "I have to save history. And even if my parents are SQ, I still have to save them."

Riq flinched with surprise, turning his head toward Sera, but this time she wouldn't meet his eyes.

"Can you?" Tilda asked. "How can you possibly save them from me?"

Sera slumped in her seat. For all they had been through, all they had done, Tilda's question sat like a weight on Sera's chest. She wasn't sure that anything could save her and Riq, her parents, or the entire world from what Tilda was about to do.

The Plan Falls Apart

IT WAS late when the knock came to Colonel Von Roenne's office. When he heard it, Dak was on the floor in the corner of the room, sorting papers for filing, and trying very hard not to stop and read the pages full of fascinating history. As the man entered, Dak knew immediately who it was: Major Kuhlenthal.

Dak knew about the major from the many history books he'd read on World War II. Following Kuhlenthal's identification of Mincemeat Man as a fraud, he had been selected as one of Hitler's top officers. From that new position, the SQ had been able to manipulate him to get everything they wanted. He had gone on to destroy the Allies in future battles at Normandy and Russia, and even helped defeat the U.S. Marines as far away as Iwo Jima in Japan.

But here, in 1943, Major Kuhlenthal was still a mid-level spy delivering his report on Mincemeat Man to his superiors. If Sera and Riq had done their jobs, then Kuhlenthal believed Major Martin was real and would recommend pulling military forces out of Sicily to defend Greece. It would then be up to Dak to ensure that Germany followed Kuhlenthal's advice. But if Sera and Riq had failed, there would be little Dak could do to persuade anyone otherwise.

Dak stood when Kuhlenthal entered the room and the two men exchanged a "Heil Hitler" with their outstretched right arms. When Kuhlenthal was ordered at ease, Dak quickly knelt down again to continue his work on the files. He hoped Von Roenne had forgotten about him, or at least wouldn't make him leave. He hadn't seen Cleo and Anton for a while, but then he hadn't exactly left this room either. He knew they were out there somewhere, looking for a way to get him.

While glaring at Dak, Kuhlenthal said to Von Roenne, "I have the news we've been waiting for. Perhaps we should discuss it privately."

"He's a child," Von Roenne said dismissively, retaking his seat. "And he has much to learn from me. Let's have the news at once. The Führer is becoming anxious."

"He should be anxious," Kuhlenthal said. "The rumors you've heard are true. The Allied target isn't Sicily. It's Greece."

Dak's ears perked up — literally; he thought they might have risen a little higher, like a dog's — but he kept his head bent low and continued working. Kuhlenthal handed Von Roenne a folder and then sat across the desk from him.

There was silence while Von Roenne filed through the papers, and Dak saw from the corner of his eye that several photos were included, too. To his curious brain, not being able to look at the photos was torture. It was like putting a chef in a gourmet restaurant and telling him not to taste the food.

With his eyes still on the report in front of him, Von Roenne said, "Is there any chance the British will know we've seen these papers?"

"None." Kuhlenthal smiled, pleased with himself. "They'll have their papers back tomorrow in their original condition and will never know we have copies. I could fool them with one eye shut."

"The British aren't stupid," Von Roenne scolded. "With both eyes open, tell me if this Major Martin is real."

Kuhlenthal sat up even straighter. "I can assure you, sir. Major Martin is a drowned British officer who was carrying top secret military plans. My report is a guarantee of Germany's success in this war!"

If he had meant to impress Von Roenne with that speech, he was going to be disappointed. Dak heard the Colonel "hmph" and turn to another page.

"Your report says survivors of the crash are being interrogated?" he asked. "Interesting."

Dak smirked. There were no other survivors, because

there had never been a plane crash. Kuhlenthal was exaggerating, probably in the hope of making his report more believable.

Eventually, Von Roenne closed the report and handed it back to Kuhlenthal. "Very well. I am sure you'll show that report to the other officers here. I will send my recommendation to the Führer by tomorrow morning."

Kuhlenthal stood, but did not leave. When he had the colonel's attention, he said, "Sir, the Führer will listen to your advice more than anyone's. He wants good news from us, not bad. If the report is true, then we will have a major victory against the Allies."

"The Führer wants *accurate* news from us," Von Roenne said sharply. "That is our duty, and nothing more."

"Yes, Colonel." Kuhlenthal saluted, tucked the report under his arm, and then left, closing the door behind him.

As soon as he'd left, Von Roenne leaned back in his chair and pressed his fingers to his temples as if a headache had come on. Dak could understand that. Ten minutes in Kuhlenthal's company and he had a headache, too.

"I know you overheard that," Von Roenne muttered to Dak. "You say that you know a lot about history. So, tell me: Is this real? Or is this a Trojan horse? A way for the British to fool us as they plan to invade Sicily?"

Dak stood and shoved his hands in his pockets. He felt a little torn in what he should say. He had grown to like Colonel Von Roenne. If Von Roenne gave bad advice to Hitler, he would have to pay the consequences. But Dak reminded himself that Von Roenne was still a Nazi, still on the wrong side of this war, and that as a spy, it was Dak's job to ignore his feelings and complete the mission. If Germany left Sicily, thousands of lives could be saved in this war, not to mention saving Earth from the Cataclysm.

"Well, what should I advise?" Von Roenne asked. "How will my choice tonight be remembered by history?"

"History teaches us that people who make the brave choices are heroes." Dak sat up straighter. "We study history to know the stories of those who stood face-to-face with real villains and won. We study history so that when it's time for us to make the hard choice, we'll know that we can do it, too."

Silence fell in the room for a moment. Dak thought about how he'd felt as they traveled through time, changing history, in some cases totally reversing the way things would be remembered. He'd felt more and more off-balance to realize that so much of what he knew, or thought he knew, about history would be different once he returned home.

"That was quite a speech," Von Roenne said softly.

"The past is easy for me," Dak said. "It's knowing the future that gives me trouble."

But then it hit him. History wasn't just about understanding the past. It was about understanding the future, *his* future. It was about having the tools to shape the future. And all he had to know was that when it came time for him to make choices, he would make the heroic choice, just as the greatest people throughout history had done. No matter what changed in the past, his future hadn't yet been written. He had to shape it, bit by bit.

With the right choices, the Cataclysm could still be avoided. Sera could bring her parents back, he could save his parents within the time warp, and Riq could — well, Riq could do whatever it was that Riq did.

"Fear makes the wolf bigger than he is," Von Roenne said. "It's an old German saying."

The image of Adolf Hitler's face came to Dak's mind. Hitler called himself the wolf. He wanted people to be afraid of him, to make the weaker choice.

"Germany should move its forces to Greece," Dak finally said. "That's what you should recommend."

"But there's only one problem," Von Roenne said. "Major Martin's papers are fakes. I know it, and I have a feeling that you know it, too."

Dak felt as stunned as if Von Roenne had hit him. But before he could speak, Von Roenne said, "There's a bright light shining in my windows; I think a car outside has left its lights on. Go close the curtains."

Dak shuffled toward the window, walking slowly

to give himself a chance to think what he should say next. When he came to the window, the lights of the car turned off, allowing Dak to see the people on the grass below.

Sera and Riq were there, staring up at him with their hands tied behind their backs. Cleo and Anton stood directly behind them, looking far too eager to cause some damage. And getting out of the car was Tilda. She brushed a hand down Sera's hair, which would've looked motherly if Sera hadn't flinched and batted Tilda's hand away with her shoulder. When she saw Dak staring down at them, Tilda pointed directly at him. Her index finger signaled him to come down to her, and the expression in her hollow eyes was perfectly clear. Either Dak would make an appearance right then to Tilda, or Sera and Riq were mincemeat.

Tilda and the Time Machine

"I'LL GET you that tea," Dak said as he started to leave Von Roenne's office.

"What tea?"

"You asked for some tea like three hours ago. I'll go get it now."

Von Roenne called after him, but Dak was already halfway down the hall, then racing down the stairs and out the door. He jogged across the lawn, stopping far enough from the group that he could talk to them without being seized.

Riq shook his head when he saw Dak coming, but Sera looked relieved. At the moment, Dak wasn't entirely sure if he had made the right decision by coming out here. Obviously, he had to help his friends, but maybe he should've thought of some cool rescue plan first, like swooping in from above, snatching them in his arms, and flying away.

On second thought, a plan like that would've

required superpowers, which were hard to come by. He'd have to trust in his ability to improvise.

"Menacing, interfering kids!" Tilda said. "We are so close to controlling both sides in this war. Don't you know how important this night is for the SQ?"

Dak rolled his eyes. Well, duh, obviously he knew.

"Don't you know how important this night is for the Hystorians?" he countered. "After tonight, the SQ will be on the road to collapse."

Tilda laughed. "The SQ is more powerful than ever right now, thanks to you!"

Dak's eyes darted to Sera, who still had the Infinity Ring's sack around her waist. So Tilda didn't have it . . . yet.

Tilda walked over to Dak. "We're going back inside those headquarters now. You're going to tell Colonel Von Roenne that you've been spying on him and that Mincemeat Man is a lie. You will do this, or you know what'll happen to your friends."

"No," Riq said. "Save history, not me. It's okay, Dak. I'm a Hystorian." Beside him, Sera nodded, and Dak couldn't have been prouder in that moment to have them for friends.

"We're all Hystorians," Dak said. "And I won't help you now."

"Yes, you will!" Angrily, Tilda grabbed Dak's arm.

Something happened when she did. Something he had experienced only once before, when he and Sera had returned to the future. Almost as if a bolt of electricity had shot through him, Dak collapsed to the ground, shivering with cold and nearly incoherent.

Somewhere in the background, he heard Sera scream. Tilda stood over him like a drooling attack dog, shouting to the others that it was only a Remnant and it would pass.

She was right about that. The pain was already receding, the worst of the icy chills. But he was still shivering and still left with the horrible feeling that the Cataclysm was coming sooner than ever. Somehow, he knew that Tilda was right—the SQ had the upper hand now. He didn't understand how that could be possible, but the one thing he was certain about made his blood run cold:

Dak's Remnant was the knowledge that the destruction of the world was his fault.

∞

By the time Dak gathered his wits, he was being carried into headquarters over Anton's shoulder. His hands were tied behind his back just as Sera's and Riq's were. Tilda and Cleo were marching on either side of him, with Riq and Sera just ahead. He didn't remember anyone deciding they should all go inside together, but he was glad they had. Whatever was going to happen next, he wanted Riq and Sera with him. If they succeeded or failed, they would do it together.

Cleo led them to a room near the kitchen, which

she said wouldn't be in use this time of night. They went inside, and Anton dumped Dak on the floor, then ordered Riq and Sera to sit beside him. Sera pressed her shoulder against his in a sign of sympathy, and Riq gave him a bump in the ribs with his elbow. He felt better just having them around.

"Fetch Colonel Von Roenne," Tilda ordered Cleo and Anton. "Whether Dak confesses or not, I can give him the evidence of their interference."

There wasn't much Dak could say to that. Tilda could easily prove they had interfered with this time line, and Von Roenne obviously wouldn't betray his own country to help him.

Colonel Alexis Von Roenne. Maybe in a strange way, the Remnant had started to clear Dak's mind. Wiped it clean of everything, except for what he needed to know to finish this mission. Suddenly, Dak knew that name's place in history.

With Cleo and Anton on their errand, Tilda found a chair and sat cross-legged on it. She withdrew a hand grenade and tossed it from one hand to the other in a way that made him nervous. Those things weren't toys.

"Blow us up now and you'll go with us," Riq said.

"Give me some credit," Tilda snapped. "I know how to use a grenade." But she stopped tossing it between her hands.

"In World War Two, the Americans designed a grenade about the size of a baseball." The fact spilled from Dak's mouth before he could stop himself. "They figured since any American boy could throw a baseball, he could throw a grenade, too."

"I've never played baseball," Tilda said.

"What a shocker," Sera whispered.

Tilda glared at them, then said, "Things may go easier for you if you confess to the colonel. Maybe it will only be the concentration camps instead of your executions."

"The concentration camps were just a slower form of execution," Dak said.

Tilda nodded. "They were. But they are only the beginning if the SQ takes control of this war. Just imagine the possibilities."

"Even you couldn't be that cruel," Sera said.

"Are you sure?" Tilda laughed. "Do you want to know how cruel I can be? Cruel enough to take a mother and father from their infant daughter and enjoy the fact that she will grow up never knowing them. I wish you could ask your parents about that day, Sera. But I'm afraid you'll never have the chance."

Beside him, Dak felt the muscles in Sera's arm tighten, but she said nothing.

"Why would you take them?" Dak asked. "If they were loyal SQ—"

"I never said they were loyal!" Tilda snapped. "But the SQ has them again, and you will never see them. Not alive anyway."

"You'd better let them go," Dak yelled. "Or I'll—"

"Or you'll what? Time travel somewhere? You can't even get the hang of it well enough to find your own parents." Tilda's grin turned wicked. "But I know where they are. They have no idea what's coming for them next. But I do."

Dak squirmed. How could Tilda talk so confidently about time travel? Maybe she had gotten back to 1943 with their Infinity Ring, but she couldn't go anywhere else. However, she didn't seem to think she was stuck here at all.

Sera had the answer. "You have your own Infinity Ring, don't you?"

Riq and Dak exchanged glances, both raising eyebrows to the other. But Sera remained focused on Tilda.

"You knew where I'd hidden our Infinity Ring and you broke into the locker," Sera said. "You used a strand of my hair to trick the device's DNA detector, and then must've gone back to the future to have the SQ replicate our Infinity Ring."

"I prefer to call it the Eternity Ring, actually," Tilda said. "Regardless, it took us months. The technology was more complicated than we had expected. We're surprised a girl of your age can operate it."

"Never underestimate a girl who knows science," Sera said. "Or for that matter, a history or language genius either."

For the first time, Riq spoke up. "Once you had your own Infinity Ring, you returned ours to the very same place and time we had left it. But why? You could've just kept ours and stranded us here."

Tilda nodded at Sera. "We wanted to see where you would go next, follow you through history and destroy the Hystorians one by one. Unfortunately, you figured out our plan, so I'm afraid it'll have to change. Your journey through time ends tonight . . . permanently."

"If that's the case, I figure we have nothing to lose," Riq said. And before Dak was fully aware of what was happening, Riq slid his tied hands under his body and was on his feet, rushing at Tilda.

Sera joined in. Her hands were still behind her, but she got in a good kick that toppled Tilda's chair over backward. The grenade that had been in her hands rolled into a corner. For his part, Dak tried doing the same move as Riq, but his hands got caught between his legs, which forced him to hunch over and hop around like some sort of deranged rabbit.

Caught off guard, Tilda toppled over on the floor. Sera knelt on one of the woman's arms, pinning it down, and Riq wrested a purse away from Tilda's other arm. After a little more hopping, Dak got his arms entirely in front of him and rushed to join his friends. Riq pulled the new Infinity Ring—the Eternity Ring—from Tilda's purse, causing her to yell in anger. She clutched at Riq, leaving a nasty scratch up his arm. But he grabbed her hand and kicked the Ring toward Dak.

"Destroy it!" Riq yelled. "Smash it, Dak!"

The Eternity Ring was made of a blue metal and glowed wherever someone grabbed on to it. But in all other ways, it seemed to be the same as the original one. Dak picked up Tilda's Ring and ran to a corner of the room, where he began hitting it against the ground. It dented and a screw wobbled in place, but the thing was built pretty solid. That figured. The SQ finally made a quality product, and it was the one thing he needed to break!

He raised up his arms again and hurled the Eternity Ring onto the ground with all his strength. He heard a crash of glass, but then Tilda rose up and grabbed him around the throat. Riq and Sera were fighting her from behind, but Tilda was much stronger than she looked and was holding her own against the three kids.

If he could only get the grenade, he could affix it to the device and warp it away. That would destroy it. But Tilda was still choking him, and the room around him was starting to fade.

"Stop this!" a voice commanded.

Everyone froze and turned to look at Von Roenne standing in the doorway with Cleo and Anton ahead of him, and two Nazi soldiers at his sides.

Dak, Sera, and Riq scooted to the other side of the room as Cleo and Anton rushed to Tilda and Von Roenne stepped inside. His face was a deep shade of red and his chest heaved with anger. "Somebody explain this to me at once!"

Tilda spoke first. "These children attacked me."

"Did they? And whose weapon is this?" Von Roenne bent over and picked the grenade up off the floor, then carefully handed it to one of the soldiers.

Tilda looked insulted at that, but only said, "I was trying to hold them here for arrest while my friends went to find you."

"Arrest?" Von Roenne said. "On what charge?"

"Spying," Anton said. "Colonel Von Roenne, we've been after Dak since the moment he wormed his way inside this building. He's working for the British."

"Not true!" Dak said. Okay, yes, he was spying, but not for the British. He was working for the Hystorians.

"This other boy and girl are spies, too," Cleo said. "The boy was in Britain, helping translate languages."

"Translate this," Riq said defiantly. *"Jus pasmirsti kaip supuvusia surio!"*

Dak chuckled as his decoder picked up the phrase spoken in Lithuanian, which said, "You stink like rotten cheese!" Even if he kind of thought of that as a compliment, he knew Cleo wouldn't.

But she ignored Riq and pointed to Sera. "And this girl was in Spain, attempting to convince your spies that the body of Major Martin is that of a real British officer."

Von Roenne raised an eyebrow. "Ah, I heard about you. You children all work together, then?"

"We're on the right side of history," Dak said. "Are you?"

Without answering, Von Roenne turned to Cleo and Anton. "You captured these spies. What do you want in reward?"

They looked at each other. Anton cleared his throat and then said, "We represent an organization that has existed for hundreds of years and stretches all over this world. In exchange for capturing these spies, we want a meeting with your Führer. He needs to know how things are going to work between us from now on."

"Then you are not Nazis?" Von Roenne asked.

"We don't have time for this!" Tilda said. "Let's just go!"

But Anton was already speaking. "We are greater than the Nazis, more powerful. We will be around long after you're gone. We are the SQ, and our time has come at last!"

25

Von Roenne's Choice

SERA WAS horrified at the thought of the SQ taking over the world here. She knew their organization was already in place wherever history was happening, and if Tilda had an Infinity Ring, their ability to create destruction whenever they wanted was far greater now.

Von Roenne seemed less impressed by Anton's posturing. "I don't know the SQ's power," he said, "but I do know ours." He turned to address the two Nazi soldiers with him. "Take these two away for questioning."

Cleo and Anton darted for the door in an attempt to escape, but the soldiers pressed them against the wall and placed them in handcuffs. Sera wasn't sure which was louder as they left, Cleo's wailing or Anton's yelling.

"Now, about you." Von Roenne turned to Tilda's corner of the room. Then he stopped. "But . . . where has she gone?"

Dak, Sera, and Riq looked the same way. Tilda had vanished. So had her Eternity Ring. Drops of amber liquid were on the ground—the fuel that powered the

Rings. Wherever she had gone, she wouldn't get far unless she could get more fuel. But she had definitely left 1943 Germany. And was no doubt already at work on the next phase of her plan.

Von Roenne's eyes narrowed, and he closed the door behind him. "You are no ordinary spies, correct?"

"We're not spies at all," Riq said. "Just travelers, trying to be sure that history goes the way it should."

"Ah, there's that word *history* again." Von Roenne turned to Dak. "And when you say you are a historian, there's something more to that word, too, I assume."

"The way we think of Hystorians, yes, sir," Dak said.

"I have already heard from other officers who have seen Major Kuhlenthal's report. Most of them believe everything he says. Hitler has asked for my opinion now, to tip the scales in either direction."

Sera frowned. "Hitler trusts you that much?"

"Yes!" Dak piped up. There was a light in his eye that Sera recognized. Dak had remembered another history fact. "He trusts you, even with his own life, Colonel—you know he does. Or, um, you *will* know that he does, eventually."

"What do you mean?" Von Roenne asked.

"I know now why it's been so hard for me to remember who you are, sir. It's because you wanted to be forgotten. You've tried to do what you think is right and hope nobody notices—because doing what's *right* can sometimes be very dangerous."

Von Roenne's eyes shifted. "What danger?"

Dak sighed. "You believe in Germany, but not in Adolf Hitler, and certainly not the horrible things he's doing in this war. In your own way, you're a spy, too."

"How dare you—"

"There are a lot of good Germans who don't like what is happening here. You're one of them. There's a secret movement to overthrow the Nazis from within. And you're a part of it, aren't you?"

Von Roenne's eyes softened. "I only wish to save lives. Thousands have already died needlessly."

Dak walked over to Von Roenne. "Just as you want to save lives, my friends and I are trying to save history. We both have to do what we know is right. Colonel, you must do the right thing with Major Kuhlenthal's report."

"Germany must leave Sicily undefended," Von Roenne whispered. "I must convince Hitler to move our armies to Greece, even though I know the Allies are on their way to Sicily."

"Yes, sir," Dak said.

"And how will history remember me for this?" Von Roenne asked. "You talk as if you already know."

"History will say you were one of the rare men to stare evil in its face and refuse to back down," Dak said. "They will call you a hero."

A knock came to the door and everyone turned. "Colonel Von Roenne," the voice on the other side said. "The Führer has requested you come to meet with him at once."

Von Roenne smiled at Dak, Sera, and Riq. Then he turned to face the door and said, "Tell him I am on my way. I have good news."

Sera later wondered what his expression was when he looked back their way again to say good-bye. She would never know for sure, because by that time, the three of them had already warped away.

26

The Sicily Aftermath

SERA, RIQ, and Dak squeezed from the warp like toothpaste from the tube. They each lay on the ground for a few minutes, recovering from the pinch of time. Gradually, Riq realized they were on sand, and that the sounds of waves crashing onto shore weren't far away. It was perfectly warm and, wherever they were, he was in no hurry to leave.

"I really hate time travel," Dak said. "Does anyone else feel like their head was stepped on by a giant?"

"Your head looks like it was." Riq grinned when he said it, but in truth, his entire body felt that same way. He shook out his hands and feet, hoping to get the blood moving again.

Sera groaned as she pulled into a sitting position. "I have an idea, Dak. Let's go forward in time to when your parents invented this stupid thing and tell them to create more *comfortable* time travel."

"Comfort. So *that's* the missing piece," Dak said.

Eventually, he rolled to his side and pushed himself up beside her. "When are we, dudes?"

Sera pointed across the sea to an island where British and American flags could be seen, even from here. "That's Sicily."

"Oh, yeah?" Riq sat beside her. "So, the Allies took the island?"

"What year is it?" Dak asked.

"Still 1943," Sera said. "But I sent us forward only a month or two, just to be sure Tilda didn't ruin anything after we left."

Riq got to his feet and wandered to a beachside garbage can. A wadded-up newspaper was inside, right on the top. It had a little sauce on it from whoever had used it to wrap their lunch, but was mostly still readable. Well, readable for anyone who was fluent in Italian. Riq smiled. He'd had that language down while other kids were still learning their ABCs.

Dak looked over his shoulder and pointed out the one word he could read: *Mussolini.* "Dictator of Italy," Dak said. "This should be interesting."

Riq spread the newspaper's front page out flat while Dak and Sera found rocks to hold it down against the breeze. The date across the top read July 25, 1943. Riq cleared his throat and translated the headline: *"After Failure in Sicily, Mussolini Arrested, Forced to Resign."*

"So Hitler lost his closest ally," Dak said. "Losing him will be a huge blow to Germany."

They bumped heads together while Riq continued translating the article for his friends. The Allied attack on Sicily was described as the largest water invasion in history. The article also suggested Germany's defeat was even bigger than the Allies ever hoped for. Once they believed the Mincemeat Man trick, Germany had moved most of its troops over to Greece. Many of the soldiers who remained on Sicily were old, untrained, and cared more about fettuccine than fighting. On the first day of invasion, over a hundred thousand Allied troops had landed on Sicily, and many of the enemy soldiers didn't even fire a single shot before surrendering. By the time Germany realized what was happening and sent reinforcements back to Sicily, the Allies had a firm hold on the island. Germany had lost one of its most important bases in the war. Better still, with Mussolini gone, many people believed Italy would begin fighting for the Allies.

The article went on to say that back in Germany, everyone was looking for someone to blame for this disaster.

"Look for Von Roenne's name," Dak said.

Riq scanned the article. He found Clauss, whom Sera explained had initially tried to sit in on Major Martin's postmortem examination. He was facing some sort of discipline. So was Kuhlenthal, although he passed the blame back to Clauss. At least with this embarrassment, he'd never rise any further in power. Von Roenne's name was briefly mentioned, but he said it was obvious the British plans had changed from what was written in Major Martin's documents.

"He's safe for a while," Riq said. "Hitler won't know he lied."

"Von Roenne isn't finished in this war," Dak said. "The things he'll do are going to save many more lives. He'll be arrested before the war ends, but he'll die as a hero."

Riq thought about that for a moment. Von Roenne knew his place in history and didn't run from it. He respected the colonel for that and hoped if he were ever called upon to do something truly great, he'd have the courage to stand and face it, too.

In his own way, maybe he already had.

"What's the caption under this picture?" Sera pointed to a picture of German tanks that appeared to be in retreat.

Riq scanned the words, and then said, "Hitler is pulling back from planned attacks in other places."

"I'll bet that after Mincemeat Man, he doesn't know what to trust anymore," she said.

"Well, history did it again!" Dak said happily. "A future spy novelist dreams up an idea for a dead body, it's all put together by a few dedicated people in a crowded basement room, and it ends up changing the course of an entire war."

"Changing history," Sera said. "We did it!"

"Hopefully, it'll stay that way," Riq said. "Don't forget Tilda has a Ring now."

"Unless she finds a way to save the rest of the fuel, she won't get far," Dak said. "I don't think we'll see her again." He stood, brushed off his pants, and added, "Who's ready for some more adventure? When are we going next?"

Sera pulled out the SQuare and punched in a few buttons, then looked up and smiled. "Looks like we'll be seeing some old friends. Who's ready for a return trip to Paris?"

EPILOGUE

TILDA LANDED in her new time with a hard thump to her right shoulder. It stung for a moment until she remembered that pain was for the weak.

Beside her, the Eternity Ring had landed on a rock and was still humming. Not a good sign. That brat, Dak Smyth, had hit it hard, though at least it got her this far. The thing was leaking fuel, but if she kept it upright, she would have enough to do what must be done.

She picked up the Ring and noticed a shining coin on the ground nearby. The money she carried in her pockets would be worthless here, so even this single coin was helpful. Upon the coin was an image of the Greek goddess Athena—a good sign she was in the right place.

Tilda sat up and pulled a bedsheet from her purse and wrapped it around herself, then hid the Ring in its folds. Voices were coming, and she saw no need to invite questions from the locals.

"Well, howdy-do," a man said, walking over to her. "Do you need help, ma'am?"

The woman with him seemed startled by Tilda's appearance. At first, Tilda thought it was because the woman recognized her, but then she remembered this man and woman had never seen her before. The woman came closer, and they both helped Tilda to her feet.

Tilda smiled and thanked them with as much kindness as her oily voice could muster.

"Are you hurt?" the man asked. "We can help you get into town if you'd like."

"Yes, please." Tilda even bent over slightly to make herself look weak. In truth, she was holding the Eternity Ring to her chest and didn't want it to be noticed. Not by these two.

As humble as she looked now, on the inside, Tilda was practically screeching with laughter. This would turn out to be the greatest joke of all time and yet she couldn't share it with anyone . . . yet.

However, by the time Dak came to this time period, she'd be ready to let him know all about it. Only, he wouldn't end up laughing at all.

The couple helping Tilda was Mr. and Mrs. Smyth, Dak's parents. They were her ticket to revenge against Dak, Sera, and Riq. And to controlling time travel forever.

Tilda's fun had only just begun.

Infinity Ring • Episode 6

Queen Marie Antoinette has hidden Paris's great works of art around the city. You must uncover her secrets to find the treasures.

Discover the mysteries of Notre Dame!

Break into the SQ strongholds!

The entire adventure unfolds in the Infinity Ring game. Log on now to live history.

Fix the past. Save the future.

Infinity Ring • BOOK 7

At last! Dak, Sera, and Riq travel back to where it all began. But they are not the only time travelers in Ancient Greece. Don't miss history in the breaking!

Includes an all-new, top secret Hystorian's Guide — which unlocks the next episode of the Infinity Ring game.

Fix the past. Save the future.